The snowman didn't stand a chance against the twins.

Now, wrapped in a scarf and mittens, Lily stepped into the snow to help.

"So they talked you into it?" Carson's deep voice danced along her nerve endings.

She held up her camera. "I thought I'd take some family photos."

"If you're sure…" He looked at her just a little longer than was necessary and she felt a strange sensation. It must be the Christmas season that was giving her these odd feelings about Carson. She never got fluttery around a man.

As Carson lifted the girls to place the snowman's hat, Lily snapped photos.

"Miss Lily, let Daddy take your picture with us!"

She glanced at Carson to see him looking at her with his head cocked. Before she could measure that look, she was kneeling beside the snowman, the twins at her sides. They were irresistible, these two sweethearts.

And so was their dad.

Too bad one little secret stood between them. An insurmountable barrier.

Or was it?

Lee Tobin McClain read *Gone with the Wind* in the third grade and has been a hopeless romantic ever since. When she's not writing angst-filled love stories with happy endings, she's getting inspiration from her church singles group, her gymnastics-obsessed teenage daughter and her rescue dog and cat. In her day job, Lee gets to encourage aspiring romance writers in Seton Hill University's low-residency MFA program. Visit her at leetobinmcclain.com.

Books by Lee Tobin McClain

Love Inspired

Redemption Ranch

The Soldier's Redemption
The Twins' Family Christmas

Rescue River

Engaged to the Single Mom
His Secret Child
Small-Town Nanny
The Soldier and the Single Mom
The Soldier's Secret Child
A Family for Easter

Christmas Twins

Secret Christmas Twins

Lone Star Cowboy League: Boys Ranch

The Nanny's Texas Christmas

The Twins' Family Christmas

Lee Tobin McClain

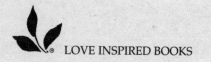

LOVE INSPIRED BOOKS

Recycling programs
for this product may
not exist in your area.

ISBN-13: 978-1-335-50984-0

The Twins' Family Christmas

Copyright © 2018 by Lee Tobin McClain

www.Harlequin.com

Printed in U.S.A.

For now we see through a glass, darkly; but then face to face: now I know in part; but then shall I know even as also I am known.
—*1 Corinthians* 13:12

To Kathy, Colleen and Sally, who helped me
brainstorm this story, and to Bill,
for research assistance and emotional support.
You guys are the best.

Chapter One

❧

You can do this.

Lily Watkins forced a smile as she carried the last of her photography gear into Redemption Ranch's Cabin Four and then came back out onto the small front porch. "Honestly, I'm fine being alone on Christmas," she said to her aunt. Which was true; at twenty-six, she'd already spent a fair number of holidays alone. "It'll be peaceful. Just what I need to finish my project."

The harder task would be to find out whether her fallen comrade's kids were being mistreated by their manipulative, cruel father. Doing that, according to her army therapist, might bring her some measure of peace.

She just had to figure out how to investigate the status of Pam's kids without losing her cool.

"I know several people in town who'd love to have you join them for Christmas dinner." Aunt Penny pulled out her phone. "Want me to make some calls?"

She *did* need to go down into the town of Esperanza Springs, talk to people, in order to find out the truth about Pam's husband and kids. But Christmas dinner wasn't the time to do that. And although she needed to make new friends and get on with her life, she wasn't likely to settle here in Colorado.

"No, thanks," she said. "I appreciate the offer, and I appreciate your letting me stay. The place is lovely, and I've been so busy. I'll enjoy a little solitude, to be honest."

To her relief, her aunt, who owned the ranch for struggling veterans and senior dogs, didn't put up a fight. "You're doing me a favor, too, taking on that other little photography project I mentioned. Anyway, the cabin's nothing fancy, but the scenery is nice."

"It's gorgeous," Lily agreed, looking out toward the snow-covered Sangre de Cristo Mountains towering over the wide, flat valley where the ranch was situated. "I can't wait to explore."

"One of our older veterans will be here over the holidays, and a couple of volunteers will stop by to take care of the dogs. They can help you with anything you need."

"I'll be fine." Lily smiled at the older woman. She was glad to have reconnected with Penny; they didn't know each other well, since Lily had grown up across the country, but in their few interactions, the older woman had always been down-to-earth and kind.

"I admire you, going back to school as a veteran and working so hard at it. And I'm thrilled you're using our ranch for your capstone project. Who knows, it might get us some great PR." She hesitated and then spoke again. "I've always regretted not doing more for you when you were a kid. Your mom wasn't the easiest to live with, and holidays stressed her out. No wonder you'd just as soon spend Christmas alone."

Lily waved a hand. "I wasn't any too easy to live with, either. I was wild."

"I know, I heard the stories." Her aunt chuckled, and then her face got serious again. "Just one more concern, and then I'll stop mother-henning you. Your car isn't really made for Colorado roads. The weather's nice now, but I saw where we might get some freezing rain tonight, in front of some snow."

Lily bit her lip, glancing over at her old car. Having spent the past year in Phoenix—and the years before that in the Middle East—she'd lost the knack for driving on icy roads. But she had to be able to get into town to investigate Pam's husband. That was the key reason she was here.

Penny patted her shoulder. "Long John—that's the vet I mentioned—can arrange a ride for you if you want to go down to town for Christmas Eve services."

"Thank you." It *would* be tough to miss church on Christmas Eve. "I might just have him do that."

"Good." Penny turned toward her car, and Lily walked with her into the frosty cold. "While you're enjoying some mountain solitude, I'll be with my daughter and grandson out east." She gave a wry smile. "I wish I could invite you to join us, but my daughter and I have a shaky relationship. Say a prayer that we'll all get along, will you?"

"Of course." Lily understood family problems all too well. She hugged the older woman. "I hope you have a wonderful time."

"I'll try." Penny got in her car, started it up and waved. Halfway down the short driveway, she stopped and lowered the window. "I forgot to tell you the name of that family you're to photograph. It's Carson Blair, one of our local pastors, and his twin six-year-olds. They'll be staying up here for the week." She raised the window and was off.

Lily stared after her aunt's car as the name she'd thrown out so casually whirled tornado-like through her head.

Carson Blair? She was doing family photographs of Carson Blair?

Pam's husband and kids were staying up here at Redemption Ranch?

The thought practically made her hyperventilate, but maybe it was a good thing. If they were staying here, it should be easy to do some quiet investigating.

She owed it to Pam. Paying that debt might help Lily move on.

She just had to make sure Carson didn't discover the awful truth about Pam's death.

Carson Blair whistled as he turned his truck into Redemption Ranch, a mere ten miles from his home in Esperanza Springs, but worlds away from his too-busy life. His last-minute plan to spend Christmas week up here was an opportunity to fill his daughters' hearts while they were off from school, let them have plenty of Daddy time. He would preach the Christmas Eve service tomorrow night, but that was all. Canceling the few other events and closing down the building meant that everyone—the secretary, the janitor, the committee members and volunteers—could do as he was doing: focus on their families.

Coming early to the ranch also let him escape the

numerous invitations a single pastor got for Christmas parties and dinners. He loved his congregation, but spending time with their big, happy extended families was a painful reminder of the life he'd hoped his girls would have, but that he hadn't been able to provide.

He had to admit that he probably wouldn't have made this Christmas getaway happen without his friend Penny's urging. She knew he needed a break. But she'd also given him a small side job: watch out for another cabin resident here for the holidays, Penny's niece, who'd been struggling with her readjustment to civilian life. Apparently she'd had formal counseling through the military, but Penny thought that Carson, as a pastor, could offer a different type of support.

"It's worth a try," the older woman had said. "And she's a beautiful woman. You might enjoy her company."

Carson had bitten back the uncharacteristically sharp retort that had formed in his mind: *Yeah, but will she enjoy mine? Pam didn't.*

He *really* needed a vacation from failed efforts at matchmaking.

"Just don't mention I asked you to talk to her," Penny had gone on, oblivious to Carson's inner dialogue. "She's independent."

He didn't like deception, but if it was the only way this woman, Lily, would open up, he supposed he could comply with Penny's request.

He pulled up to Cabin Two and turned to wake up the twins, both asleep in the back seat after a sugar-laden holiday party in their kindergarten class. Their identical faces were flushed, their long eyelashes resting on chubby cheeks. His chest tightened. Despite the sad ending of his wife's life, the weaknesses of his marriage—the weaknesses he'd had as a husband—his daughters were the wonderful, God-given outcome.

"Wake up, sleeping beauties," he said quietly, giving a light pat to Skye's arm, then to Sunny's.

"Is it Christmas?" Sunny jerked upright.

"Presents?" Skye asked, yawning.

Carson chuckled. His girls did know the true meaning of Christmas, but preachers' kids were like anyone else's when it came to gifts.

"Christmas is in two days," he reminded them. "We're at the ranch now, though. We're going to do some sledding, and play with the dogs, and do puzzles by the fire. Let's get our stuff into the cabin."

"Yay!" Sunny cried, and both girls scrambled out of their booster seats.

But as Carson opened the truck door, Long John McCabe, one of the gray-haired veterans who lived at the ranch, came toward him, his walker bumping over the dirt path at an alarming pace. "Change of plans," he said. "Willie's cabin had a plumbing leak, so you can't stay there. We're putting you up in Cabin Five."

Carson shrugged. "Sure, that's fine. We'll be a little farther away from you, but we can bundle up and come visit."

"Long John!" Both girls spilled out of the truck and ran to hug the older gentleman, carefully, as they'd been taught. "We have a present for you," Skye added.

"It's a—" Just in time, Sunny slapped a hand over her own mouth.

"I might have a little something for you two girls as well." Long John reached a shaky hand down to pat Skye's head, then Sunny's.

"I'm going to pull the truck down to Cabin Five so we can unload," Carson said. "Girls, hop back in."

"But we want to go pet Rockette," Skye complained.

"And see Mr. Long John's Christmas tree," Sunny added, then looked up at the older man, her forehead wrinkling. "Do you *have* a Christmas tree?"

"If you don't," Skye said, "you can come see ours, when we get it set up."

"Maybe you can come help!" Sunny suggested. "Daddy, can he?"

"I'm fine. I've got a little Norfolk Island pine in a pot." Long John chuckled at the girls' enthusiasm and waved Carson toward the row of cabins. "Go ahead, get unpacked and settled. I'll entertain these two for half an hour, maybe fix 'em some hot chocolate."

"Can we, Daddy?" Skye pleaded.

Carson drew in a breath to say no, not wanting to put Long John to the trouble, but just in time, he caught the eagerness in the older man's eyes. Long John didn't have any kids or grandkids of his own, and his worsening Parkinson's disease made it difficult for him to get out.

He glanced over at Long John's cabin and noticed an accessibility ramp in front, its raw, light-colored wood a contrast to the old cabin's dark hue. That was new.

"You girls can visit," he said. "But behave and do what Mr. Long John says."

"Yay!" Sunny ran toward Long John's cabin.

"Wait!" Skye called sharply after her twin. She walked beside Long John at a sedate pace, glancing over her shoulder to make sure that Carson had noticed her considerate behavior.

He had, of course, and he gave her a thumbs-up. It

was such a blessing, these older veterans becoming a part of his girls' lives. The twins had no local grandparents, but these men filled the gap, just as the girls filled a gap in Long John's life.

He let the truck glide down the road to Cabin Five. Got out and opened the back hatch…and stopped.

At the cabin next door, kneeling to catch a photo of the sun sinking over the Sangre de Cristos, was the most beautiful woman he'd ever seen.

Well, the second-most beautiful. He could never forget his wife's glossy golden hair, her sparkling eyes. He'd never stopped loving her, even through the arguments and the emotional distance and the absences.

He'd never *thought* he would notice another woman. But he was sure noticing this one.

Was *this* Penny's niece? If so…wow.

Clad in worn, snug-fitting jeans and a blue parka, the blonde was focusing so closely on what she was doing that she paid him no attention.

Not that a woman who looked like that would pay someone like him any attention. Pam—popular, fun-loving Pam—had been the amazing exception, the girl a former nerdy weakling would never have expected to attract.

"Daddy!" Sunny's voice sounded behind him, out of breath and upset.

He turned to see her running toward him, covering the rocky dirt road at breakneck speed. "Slow down, sweetie! What's wrong?"

"Daddy!" She hurtled into him and bounced back, grabbing his hand. "Mr. Long John is hurt!"

He dropped the bags he was carrying and turned toward Long John's cabin. "Where's Skye?"

"She's sitting with him. Come on!"

Carson ran beside her, their breath making fog clouds in the cold air. He should never have left the girls alone with a man in Long John's condition, even if he *had* seemed fine just a few minutes ago.

Running footsteps sounded behind him, then beside. "Which cabin?" the blonde woman asked. She was carrying a large first aid kit, and she lifted it to show him. "I overheard. Might be able to help."

"First one in the row." He gestured toward it.

"Daddy... I can't...run any...more." Sunny slowed beside him, panting, so he stopped to pick her up as the woman jogged ahead.

Now he could see Long John sitting on the bottom porch step, Skye beside him. The older man was conscious and upright, which was reassuring. When the blonde woman reached him, she knelt, spoke and then started pawing through her first aid kit.

Carson reached the trio a moment later and swung Sunny to the ground. "What's going on? Everyone okay?"

"I'm taking care of him," Skye said, patting Long John's arm.

"That you are, sweetie." Long John reached as if to put an arm around her and winced.

"I wouldn't move that arm just now, sir," the blonde woman said. Something about the cadence of her words spelled military. So this most likely *was* Penny's niece.

"Good point." Long John looked ruefully up at Carson. "I'm okay, it's just the Parkinson's getting worse. Affects my balance sometimes. I hit the edge of the porch wrong and went down. Bumped myself up and got a nasty splinter."

"He was spozed to use the ramp," Sunny explained, "but he didn't think he needed it."

"What's Parkinson's?" Skye asked.

"It's a disease that affects your muscles." As Long John went on with a simple explanation, Carson breathed a sigh of relief. His girls were okay, and Long John was, too, from the looks of things.

Penny's niece—Lily, her name was—had Long John's arm out of his parka and was using tweezers to remove the splinter. Once that was done, she swabbed the older man's hand with something from a clear bottle.

When she glanced back and saw Carson watching, she frowned and nodded toward the porch. "This porch isn't in great shape, especially for someone with mobility issues."

Carson nodded. "They've been gradually upgrading their structures here, as money permits. Looks like this place should move to the top of the list." The struggling ranch was getting back on its feet—they all hoped—but it would take time to recover from the embezzlement it'd suffered earlier this year.

Meanwhile, while Carson was here, he'd try his hand at shoring up Long John's old porch.

"Good idea." Lily gave him a brief smile and he sucked in his breath. No woman would ever be as beautiful as Pam, but this one, with her slim figure and short, wavy hair and lively eyes, came close.

Not that he was interested.

And certainly, not that she would be.

Carson focused back in on the conversation among Long John and his daughters.

"Could I get that disease?" Sunny was asking.

"Not likely," Long John said. "I was in a place called Vietnam, and spent a lot of time around a fancy weed killer called Agent Orange. The doctors think that might be why this happened." He waved a hand at his body. "But don't you worry. They don't use it anymore."

"I'm sorry." Skye patted his arm again, and Carson smiled.

A matching smile crossed Lily's face as she looked at the little girl comforting the old man. "There you go, sir," she said to Long John. "All patched up."

"Can I help you get inside?" Carson asked.

"Just a hand to stand up," Long John said. "Think I'll take it easy, watch a little TV. Your hot chocolate will have to wait until another day," he added to the girls.

"That's okay," Skye said, and then nudged her twin.

"That's okay," Sunny said with considerably less enthusiasm.

Carson helped Long John up on one side while Lily steadied him from the other. Once he was on his feet, he gestured for his walker. "I'll be fine from here," he said.

"But we want to see Rockette!" Sunny protested.

Bless her. That would give Carson the excuse to make sure Long John was settled inside. "We'll just visit for a minute," he said.

So he followed Long John up the ramp, the girls eager behind them, Lily bringing up the rear. Once inside, he stood ready to help the older man into his chair, but it was obviously a move he'd made many times before and he did it smoothly.

The girls joyously patted big, gray-muzzled Rockette, who licked their faces and then flopped to the floor with a big doggy sigh that made them both giggle. They settled down beside the patient old dog, patting her head and marveling over her soft ears.

"Can I make you some coffee?" Carson asked Long John, moving toward the kitchen area, basically one wall of the cabin's main room. He noticed a single bowl, glass and spoon in the dish drainer.

"Don't touch the stuff, but thanks." Long John had the remote in hand, flipping channels.

"You let us know if you need anything." Carson turned to usher the girls out and realized that Lily wasn't there. Sometime while he'd been getting Long John settled, she must have slipped away.

Sure enough, when they got outside, he saw her up the road, walking rapidly toward her cabin.

Which probably meant she didn't want to socialize. Penny had said she was independent.

But he'd promised to reach out to her. He'd get his things unloaded and then pay a little visit, do an informal assessment of his quiet neighbor.

Lily heard the little girls' voices from a distance behind her and practically ran up the steps of her cabin. She went inside and shut the door.

Pam's husband and her twins. Seeing them had tugged her emotions in ways she didn't expect. Especially those adorable, energetic little girls who were the image of their mother.

What a family Pam could have had…if only she'd survived.

But Lily needed to focus on the future rather than wallowing in regret. She needed to gather her strength and find out if Carson was, in fact, an abusive bully. The least she could do for Pam, since she couldn't turn back the clock and change what had happened, was to check on her children and make sure they were okay.

They'd seemed more than okay, but appearances could be deceiving.

She went to the window and watched as the man and the little blonde twins carried things into the cabin next door.

Hearing the laughter of the children, punctuated by some booming laughs from *him*, made loneliness squeeze Lily's stomach, but she straightened her back and drew in the deep, cleansing breath she'd learned about from her army therapist. She deserved to be lonely.

Because the father-daughter fun outside didn't make up for what was missing from the picture: a mom. Beautiful, mysterious Pam, who hadn't gotten to spend nearly enough time with her husband and kids in the years before her death.

Don't dwell on what you can't change. Lily looked away from the trio's good spirits toward Long John's cabin. She'd seen the undecorated Christmas tree, the single strand of lights around the porch railing, the pizza box beside the trash can. All of it spoke of a man alone, and Long John wasn't in such good shape.

Having a trained medic—her—up here over the holidays, when the older man was likely to be cut off from his support system, might be a blessing. Something God had planned. It was another way Lily could make up for her past.

When she looked back at the little twins, they were building something out of rocks, possibly a house for the bright collection of toys on the ground. Normally, she didn't understand kids—they were aliens to her. But these girls' serious, intent faces made her smile. They were focused on fun, just as kids should be.

Fun. It wasn't something she'd thought a lot about. No time. She'd joined the army at eighteen, gotten trained as a medic and then a combat photographer, done pretty well for a poor girl from a rough background. After that, college on the GI Bill at an accelerated pace.

Everyone told her to slow down, but she didn't want to. Slowing down gave her the time to think.

It wasn't until she heard the knock on the door that she realized the girls' father was nowhere in sight.

As she went to answer a second knock, she glanced through the window.

Carson Blair stood on her front porch. Her heart thumped, and she inhaled a bracing breath. She'd wanted to investigate the man, to make sure he was treating Pam's girls well.

It looked like the opportunity had just fallen into her lap.

Chapter Two

Carson waited for the mysterious Lily to answer his knock, wondering at his own intense curiosity.

The pastor part of him had noticed the sad, distant look in her eyes. There was some kind of pain there, and it tugged at his heart. He'd try to establish at least an initial connection. There was plenty of time to do more probing, as Penny had requested, within the next few days.

He also wanted to get a better look at her, and honesty compelled him to ask himself why. Surely not because he found her attractive? He did, of course—he was human, and she was gorgeous—but gorgeous women were not for him. He wanted to marry again, if God willed it; his girls needed a mother, and his own work as a pastor would be enhanced if he had a wife ministering at his side. Not to mention how long and lonely winter evenings could be when you didn't have a partner to talk to and love.

But this woman wasn't a prospect.

The door jerked open. "Can I help you?" came a

voice out of the cabin's dimness. A voice that wasn't exactly friendly.

"We didn't have the chance to introduce ourselves. I'm Carson Blair. Just came by to say hello, since it looks like we're going to be neighbors over the holiday."

"Pleased to meet you." Her voice didn't sound pleased. "I'm Lily. What brings you to the ranch? Penny mentioned you live nearby."

Her interrogation surprised him—in his counseling role, he needed to find out about her, not vice versa— and it made him feel oddly defensive. "My daughters and I are looking for a peaceful Christmas, away from our daily stresses and strains."

"Your girls are stressed?" She came forward into the light, standing on the threshold. Her wheat-blond hair seemed to glow, and her high cheekbones and full lips were model-pretty.

So were her big, slate-colored eyes. Eyes that glared, almost like she had it in for him.

He took a breath and reminded himself of that old counseling cliché: *hurt people hurt people.* "I guess it's just me that's stressed," he admitted, keeping his tone easy and relaxed. "Busy time of year for a pastor. But the girls are thrilled to be up here with Long John and the dogs."

Her face softened a little. "It *is* nice up here. Good feel to the place."

"Yes, there is." He paused. "Say, Penny mentioned that you're a photographer. And that she'd asked you to take some family photos of us as a Christmas present."

"That's right. When are you available?"

Noting that her body language was still tense, Carson decided that this wasn't the time to work out details. Besides, she wasn't inviting him in, and her short-sleeved shirt and faded jeans weren't cold-weather gear. She must be freezing. "We can figure that out in the next day or two. Meanwhile, if you need anything, I'm right next door."

He turned to go down the steps when two blond heads popped up next to the railing. "Hi," Sunny, always the bolder of the two, called out to Lily. "What's your name?"

Carson walked halfway down the steps and stopped in front of his curious girls. "I think Miss…" He realized he didn't know her last name. "I'm sure our neighbor is busy right now."

"Whatcha doing?" Sunny slid under the wooden rail and climbed the rest of the way up the steps. "Can we see your cabin?"

Skye, easing up the stairs behind Sunny, didn't speak, but it was plain to see that she was equally interested.

"Girls." He put a hand on each shoulder. "We don't go where we're not invited." Watching the pouts start to form, he added, "Besides, we've got unpacking to do, and then some dogs to meet."

"Dogs!" they both said at the same time, their curiosity about the lady next door forgotten.

"Unpacking first," he said, herding them down the steps. But as he turned to offer an apologetic wave to their neighbor, he thought her stance on the porch looked lonely, her eyes almost…hungry.

The next morning, Lily shivered in the bright sun, looked at the newly slick, icy road out of the ranch and had a crisis of confidence.

Could her ancient, bald-tired Camaro handle the trip into town?

If not, could she handle staying up here without coffee?

The lack of caffeine had left her head too fuzzy to figure out how to investigate her surprise neighbors, and there was no coffee or coffee maker in the cabin.

She could go to Long John or Carson to see what she could borrow, but she didn't want to open up that kind of neighborly relationship with Carson, not when she was trying to ascertain his suitability as a father. And she'd heard Long John say that he didn't drink coffee.

Her caffeine-withdrawal headache was setting in big-time. So she had to go, and now, full daylight with the sun shining, was the right time, rather than waiting until later when it was likely to snow. And when all the shops would be closed for Christmas Eve.

Because most people wanted to be with their families.

You're not an orphan; you're just making a choice. Her father was still living, and he would have certainly taken her in for Christmas. If she could find him, and if he had a roof over his head. And if he was sober.

But in all the years she'd spent Christmas with her parents as a child, she couldn't remember one where he'd made it through the holiday without heavy drinking. There was no reason to think that now, with her mother gone, this year would be an exception; the opposite, in fact.

And while she hated to think of her father being alone, she knew he probably wasn't. He was probably

carousing with his buddies. He was the friendly type
and had a ton of them.

The image of her dad's jolly face brought an unexpected tightness to her throat.

"It's her!" came a high, excited shout.

"Hey, Miss Neighbor!"

The two childish voices let her know she'd stood
reflecting too long. She turned, and the sight of the
twins—*Pam's twins*—coming toward her made her
heart turn over. Clad in identical red snow jackets,
black tights and furry boots, they could have been an
advertisement for Christmas family joy.

And she couldn't make herself turn away from
them, even though she should. She'd keep it brief.
"Good morning, ladies," she said, kneeling down to
be at their level.

They slipped and slid to her with the fearless footing of children accustomed to snow and ice. "Where
are you going?" one of them asked.

Lily studied her. "Are you Sunny?" She'd noticed
that Carson had gestured toward the twin in the lead
when naming them yesterday.

"How did you know?" Sunny asked, eyebrows lifting high.

"Nobody ever does, at first." The other little girl
studied her, head cocked to one side.

"Just a guess," she said, smiling at them. Man, were
they cute.

Man, did they look like Pam.

"Where are you going?" The quieter girl, who must
be Skye, asked.

"Down to town," Lily said.

"Us, too!" Sunny sounded amazed. "Daddy sent us

out to play so he could look over his sermon in peace, but as soon as he's done that, we're going down into town, too."

Oh, right. Pam's husband was a preacher. According to Pam, it was a cover-up for his abusive ways.

"Is your dad pretty strict?" she asked the twins. And then she wished she could take the words back. It wasn't fair to ask the girls to tattle on their father. If she wanted to know something, she would discover it by observation, not by grilling these two innocents.

"What's strict?" Sunny asked.

"She means, does Daddy make us behave." Skye glanced back at the house. "He tries to be strict, but we don't always do what he says."

Lily was dying to ask what kind of punishments he meted out, but she didn't.

Didn't need to, as it turned out.

"When we don't do what he says," Sunny said, "we get a time-out."

"Or an extra chore," Skye added.

"Yeah, we have lots of chores!" Sunny spread her arms wide and nodded vigorously, the picture of childhood overwork. "We have to make our beds *every* day."

"And put the silverware in the drawer." Skye frowned. "Only, here at the cabin, we don't have a dishwasher. So Daddy washed our dishes last night, himself, and put everything away."

Lily waited for a continuation of their onerous list of chores, but it didn't come. Either the list was limited to two not-very-challenging tasks or their attention had drifted elsewhere.

Meanwhile, she had better get going before Carson the ogre came out of the cabin. Even though she needed to check on Pam's twins, she didn't want to get sucked into even a superficial friendship. Not when she had secrets to keep. "It was nice talking to you girls," she said, getting into her car and starting it up.

The girls still stood next to her car, and Sunny's lips were moving, so she lowered her window.

"Maybe we'll see you in town," Sunny said.

"That would be...fun," Lily said. *Not.* She would drive down to town, get the coffee and coffee maker she needed now even more desperately than before— her headache was getting worse—and then drive back up and hide out in her cabin for the duration of Christmas Eve.

Spending the holiday by herself seemed a little bit lonelier after talking to Skye and Sunny, but Lily pushed the feeling away. She put the car into gear and started cautiously down the icy road.

The car picked up speed on the incline, and she hit the brake reflexively. The car fishtailed a little, even though her pace was slow. Her heart beat faster, and her hands on the cold steering wheel were slick with sweat. If she went off the road, who would help her?

You're tough; you're a soldier. She just had to remember that you braked gently in icy conditions.

She gathered her courage and took her foot off the brake. The car started moving again.

There was a shout behind her, and when she looked into the rearview mirror, she saw the two little girls running after her. That wasn't safe. What if they got too close and the car went out of control? She braked, harder this time, and the antilock *tick-tick-tick-tick* didn't stop the car from sliding sideways. It stopped

just at the edge of a two-foot dropoff. Not deadly, but...
She put the car into Park and got out just as the girls reached her.

"We saw your car slide and we told Daddy!" Sunny said.

"And he said you could ride to town with us." Skye looked up, her brown eyes round and hopeful. "We have a big truck."

"Oh, no, it's okay." She walked to the front of her car, and it was, in fact, okay. About three inches from being not okay, but okay.

She looked back toward her cabin and saw Carson Blair striding toward them, flannel-shirted and boot-clad and looking nothing like any preacher she'd ever seen.

More like a lumberjack.

Weren't there social media sites and photo calendars about good-looking lumberjacks?

She shoved *that* ridiculous notion away, her face heating as Carson reached them.

"Everything okay?" He patted each twin on the back and then walked around to look at the front of her car.

"It's fine," she said.

"But her car went sliding. Like a sled!" Sunny demonstrated with a complicated hand motion.

Carson nodded. "I like the rear-wheel-drive Camaros," he said, tapping the hood, "but they're not the greatest on snow and ice."

"I didn't think of that before I came," she admitted. "Not much snow in Phoenix. But it's no big deal for me to get to town," she added while her body cried out for caffeine.

"Daddy's a good driver," Skye said earnestly.

"You should come to town with us!" Sunny was wiggling her excitement, which seemed to be her normal state of being. "You could come to church!"

"Oh, I..." She trailed off, part of her noticing that the girls seemed enthusiastic about church and life in general, nothing like abused children were likely to be.

"You're welcome to join us," Carson said. "We're picking up a couple of things at the hardware store and going to church for Casual Christmas Eve."

That made sense of Carson's lumberjack attire and the girls' outdoorsy clothing. "Are you staying until midnight? Because I can't...can't do that." *Can't deal with you and your girls for that many hours in a row.*

Carson waved a hand and smiled, and he went instantly from good-looking to devastatingly handsome. "I scored this year. Got the afternoon service, and the other church in town—Riverside Christian—they're doing the evening services." He held out his hand. "Come on. I'll drive your car back up, and you can ride into town with us."

His comfortable, take-charge manner both put her at ease and annoyed her. It was nice to think of someone else driving on the slippery roads—and it was *really* nice to think of coffee—but she didn't know Carson. Or rather, she only knew *of* him, and none of what she'd heard from Pam was positive.

Besides, she didn't want to be that wimpy woman who needed a man to drive her around.

His hand was still out for the keys, but she held on to them.

A smile quirked the corner of his mouth. "If you want to drive it back up yourself, go for it," he said, "although I've been itching to get behind the wheel of a cherry-red Camaro since I was seventeen."

She suspected it was a ruse to make her comfortable letting him drive and help her save face. Okay, that was nice of him. She handed him the keys.

Carson was glad they ended up taking Lily to town. Beyond Penny's request, he found himself curious about the shy photographer. She said she was working on a college project, and he had surmised from all the camera equipment that it involved photography. But that was all he knew.

He was about to ask when she turned to him. "So, how long have you and the twins lived in this area?" she asked.

"We moved here when they were born," he said. "We've always lived in Colorado, various parts, but a job opened up here at just the point when we were ready for a more stable life. How about you? Where are you from?"

"Most recently, Phoenix." Lily didn't elaborate but instead asked another question. "Do you like the job?"

He got the odd feeling she was trying to ask him questions to deflect attention from herself. "I do. It's a wonderful church and community. Not without its problems—there's a lot of poverty—but people are good-hearted here. It's an old-fashioned community. Neighbors look after neighbors." Great. He sounded like his grandfather, hearty and wholesome and focused on his own small town. Not fun and exciting.

Pam had always criticized him for being boring.

But how could he not be? He'd grown up on the

straight and narrow, with strict parents. Now he was a pastor and a frazzled single dad.

What chance did he have to be full of scintillating conversation, when his biggest social activity all season had been helping at the kids' classroom holiday party?

"And how about you girls?" Lily turned in the seat to look back at them. "How do you like your town?"

"There's an ice cream store," Skye said matter-of-factly, as if that were the feature that determined the worth of a town.

"And our teacher, Ms. Garcia, is so nice." Sunny launched into her favorite theme. "She brings her dogs to school sometimes. And when we told her we want a dog, too, she said one of her dogs is having puppies!"

Not this again. "If we ever did get a dog," Carson said, "we would get one from the shelter. Not a puppy."

"That's okay, Daddy," Skye said. "We like all dogs. We don't have to get a mala… Mala…"

"Malamute?" Lily glanced over at Carson. "A malamute puppy would be adorable, but a lot of work. And hair."

"Exactly." Carson turned the truck onto Esperanza Springs's Main Street. "Look at the decorations, girls," he said in an effort to distract them from their dog quest.

It worked. Even though it was early in the afternoon, it was a gray enough day that the streetlights had lit up. The town resembled a Christmas card scene.

"So beautiful," Lily murmured, leaning forward and staring out the window, elbows on knees.

"You said you live in Phoenix?" he asked.

"Yeah." She wrinkled her nose. "We have Christmas decorations, but where I live, they tend to be giant inflatable cartoon characters and lights wrapped around the trunks of palm trees. This is prettier."

Carson pulled the truck into a parking space just down from the hardware store. Across the street, the Mountain High Bakery was doing a surprisingly brisk business—people picking up their Christmas desserts, no doubt. In front of La Boca Feliz, Valeria Perez folded the signboard and picked it up, shaking her head at an approaching couple with an apologetic smile. Closing down for the day: good. That meant Valeria would be able to attend church with the rest of her family.

"Oh, wow, look!" Sunny bounced in her seat. "Mrs. Barnes's new dog has reindeer antlers on!"

"Can we go pet it, Daddy? Can we?" Skye leaned forward to beg.

"In a minute. Get out on Lily's side." He came around and opened Lily's door. Growing up as the only child of older parents had certainly had its drawbacks, like making him into a total nerd, but at least he had learned old-fashioned manners. His women friends always praised him for that. Usually in the process of making it clear that he was just a friend, no more.

And why did that matter? He automatically held out a hand to help Lily down from the high truck seat. He didn't look at her, not wanting her to read his thoughts.

Once he'd helped her down and dropped her hand almost as fast as she pulled it away, he opened the back door of the truck. The girls tumbled out and rushed to Mrs. Barnes, an older member of the congregation known for pressing other church members into service doing things they didn't want to do. At a ranch fundraiser last summer, she had come to meddle but had ended up falling in love with one of the senior dogs. Now Bosco plodded slowly beside her, indeed sporting a pair of light-up antlers.

"Girls," he warned, a hand on each one's shoulder. "Make sure you ask Mrs. Barnes if it's okay to pet Bosco." He knew it was, but he also wanted the twins to practice safety around other people's dogs. Plus, he knew that Mrs. Barnes enjoyed talking about Bosco, reveling in the attention and status her dog brought her. Indeed, several other people had already clustered around to admire the dog in his costume.

"Dogs sure do a lot for people," Lily said, closer than he had expected.

He looked at her and saw that a smile tugged at the corner of her mouth.

"Oh, no," he said, mock-serious, "you're not going to throw me under the bus. I am *not* getting a dog."

She raised mittened hands, laughing openly now. "Did I tell you to get a dog?" she asked innocently.

Her cheeks were flushed in the cold, and strands of blond hair escaped from the furry hood of her jacket. Her lips curved upward, and her wide eyes sparkled, and Carson's heart picked up its pace.

Time to get businesslike. "The hardware store is right there," he said, gesturing toward Donegal's Hardware. "Come on, girls, let's leave Mrs. Barnes to her errands. We have a few of our own to do."

"What are you buying, Miss Lily?" Sunny tucked a hand into Lily's.

Not to be outdone, Skye took Lily's other hand.

They walked ahead of Carson, and the sight made his heart lurch.

Maybe this was a very bad idea. Carson didn't need the girls getting attached to some model-perfect photographer who would be here only a few days. He'd noticed that they tended to be drawn to young women, probably because they missed their own mother. They'd been four when she died, so their memories were patchy, but despite Carson's best efforts to be both mother and father, some part of them knew what was missing in their lives.

"I'm buying coffee and a coffee maker," Lily said, "because I love coffee so much, and there isn't one at the cabin."

"You're like our daddy!" Skye tugged at her hand. "Daddy isn't very nice if he hasn't had his coffee."

Lily laughed back at him, and he couldn't keep his own mouth from lifting into a smile. Their eyes met.

Color rose into her cheeks, and she looked away, and then the girls tugged her into the store.

Inside, tinsel and ornaments hung from the ceiling and Christmas music played. Long lines of customers waited at the two front registers, some holding wrapping paper and others bags of salt. Two men both approached the last snow shovel in a rack, and then one waved his hand in good-natured defeat. "You can have it," he said, "if you'll come over and shovel my walks when the snow starts."

"Deal," the other man said, laughing.

Lily and the twins had disappeared, so Carson took advantage of the opportunity to pick out two boxes of ornaments. They had a few, but not enough to make even their small artificial tree look as colorful as six-year-olds demanded.

Of course, Carson ran into several of his parishioners, and by the time he'd greeted them, Lily and the twins emerged from the back of the store. "Success!" Lily said, holding up a box with a coffee maker in it.

"And I have something for you." With a fake-gallant gesture, he poured her a paper cup of free, hardware-store coffee and handed it over.

"You're my hero," she said, taking the cup and inhaling appreciatively. She took a sip and her eyes met his.

He started to feel giddy.

When they reached the counter with their purchases, Marla Jones, the cashier, reached over the counter to shake Lily's hand. "So you're Penny's niece? Penny told me you were staying up at the ranch."

Lily's smile was a little shy. "I'm just here for a few days, to photograph the dogs. My senior project."

"You know," Marla said, "I'd like to talk to you about going back to school for photography. I'd really like to finish my degree, but I'm worried that I'm too old."

"You should! It's been a great experience for me. And there are lots of older students at colleges these days."

"Do you mind if I get your number? It's Liliana… what was your last name?"

"Watkins," she said.

Shock exploded like a bomb in Carson's chest. He must have made some weird sound, because she glanced over at him. When she saw his reaction, her eyes widened, and she turned quickly away.

The clerk rang up Lily's purchases, still chatting, and then punched her number into Lily's phone. Meanwhile, all the implications slammed into Carson. Lily was Liliana Watkins? Pam's party-happy roommate? The one with all the boyfriends? He shook his head, but he couldn't shake the pieces into place.

Why was Liliana at the ranch? Was she here to dry out? To bring a message from Pam? Most important, was it safe for his girls to be around her?

His eyes narrowed. Had Penny known the connection between Lily and Pam when she'd asked Carson to check on her?

Lily grabbed her purchase and her change, gave a quick, artificial smile to Marla and then hurried toward the door.

He wasn't letting her escape. "Hey, wait up," he called after her as he handed cash to Marla.

Lily hesitated, then turned.

Carson took his change and strode over to where she was standing. "I need to talk to you later, after church," he said.

"Okay." She looked pale, but she didn't ask him why. For some reason, that angered him.

The girls were calling to him, talking to Marla, collecting his bags. "I'd like to get some information from you, *Liliana*," he said, keeping his voice low, "about Pam."

Chapter Three

❧

A short while later, Lily stood in the foyer of the small church while Carson talked to a parishioner, and the girls excitedly greeted their friends.

Anxiety twisted her stomach. He knew.

Carson Blair had obviously just realized that she'd been Pam's friend and roommate, and now she had to decide how to deal. And she had to figure it out soon, before the church service ended.

Just the fact that she hadn't said anything when she'd met them made her seem guilty of wrongdoing. She should have copped to the truth right away. Should have smiled easily and said, "Hey, what a coincidence, I think I knew your wife."

But she'd kept quiet. How was she going to explain that?

Out of all the things he was likely to think and wonder about, one was the most worrisome: Did he know she'd been right there with Pam at the end? How much did he know about his wife's death?

"Come see our costume!" Little Sunny tugged at Lily's hand, bringing her back to the present. They walked farther into the small, white-adobe-fronted church building. Evergreen boughs emitted their pungent aroma, and a large Christmas tree dominated the corner of the lobby. Adults talked and laughed and hung up coats while kids ran around. From the sanctuary, a choir practiced a jazzed-up version of "Hark! The Herald Angels Sing"; the music stopped midline, there was some talk and laughter, and then the group sang the same line again and continued on.

"Over here!" Skye beckoned, and Sunny tugged, and Lily followed them down a hallway to a classroom where barely organized chaos reigned.

"We're two parts of a camel," Skye explained. "I was the front in the dress 'hearsal last week, so Sunny gets to be the front today." The contraption they held up made Lily smile; someone had affixed a brown sheet to a horse-on-a-stick, and a complicated arrangement of pillows made for the hump. Two holes allowed the girls' heads to stick up through it, creating visibility and a very odd-looking camel.

"Can you help them into it?" a young woman, obviously pregnant, called over her shoulder. She was kneeling, trying to place a flowing head covering over a shepherd boy who kept trying to twist away. "I'm Barb, by the way," she added.

"Um, sure." Lily knelt beside the twins and, despite their confusing instructions, got the costume situated on them. Immediately, they began prancing around, running into another child just as Carson appeared in the doorway.

"Skye! Sunny!" He lifted his hands in warning. "Slow down."

"Daddy!" They rushed over and struggled to embrace him, their camel costume twisting askew, as if they hadn't just parted from him ten minutes before.

Wow, he was handsome. And she'd felt a spark between them earlier, in the street, when they'd teased about getting a dog.

What was *that* all about? Getting attracted to Pam's husband was just plain wrong.

"You look great." He hugged them both quickly and readjusted their costume. "I want you to go over there and sit with the others until it's time to come out and do your show." He guided them toward the calmest corner of the room, where several other child actors milled around.

"I'm sorry things are so wild, Pastor Blair," Barb said. "I'm trying to get everyone dressed, but it's hard. We'll be ready when it's time."

"Isn't Missy here?"

She shook her head. "Her little one's sick. But I'm sure I can handle it."

"If you tell me what to do," Lily heard herself say, "I can help."

"Thank you!" Carson gave her a smile that warmed her to her toes, and then someone called him from behind. He turned toward an agitated-looking acolyte who was holding a broken candle. He spoke to her gently, and they walked off down the hall.

"I'd appreciate your help." Barb gave her a harried smile. "If you can just keep the kids entertained while I get these last couple dressed, and help me get them to the sanctuary, we'll be good."

Keep kids entertained? How did you do that? She wasn't a mom or an aunt, and she didn't have many friends with kids.

As she looked at them, her mind a blank, the group began to nudge and push one another in the small, crowded room.

Inspiration hit. "All right, we're going to take pictures," she said, pulling out her phone. "First, everyone stand up."

Like well-practiced models, they instantly struck poses, and she snapped several photos.

"Now everyone look sad."

They giggled and tried to do it without success.

"Now individual photos. Quietest kids go first."

They continued doing photo sessions, and Lily actually got some good shots that the parents would love, including candids of the kids who were still being helped into their costumes.

What seemed like only a few minutes later, a gray-haired man appeared in the doorway. "You kids are up next," he said, and the children shrieked and lined up, following Barb's harried instructions.

Once they got to the front entrance of the sanctuary, several other adults appeared to direct the children, and Barb gave Lily a quick half hug. "Thanks for giving me a hand. You can slip in and watch, if you'd like."

So Lily did, strangely warmed by the opportunity to help out.

The sight of the girls galumphing up the aisle, Sunny grinning and waving while Skye tried to hold the camel costume in place, made Lily's breath catch.

Pam would've found the camel costume hysterically funny. Lily could almost hear her friend's rollicking laugh that usually ended in an undignified snort. It would have created a disruption in church, but Pam would have enjoyed that, too, rebel that she was.

If only she could be here. If only things had gone down differently those last days before she'd died.

Lily swallowed hard and made herself focus on the service. But the past seemed determined to intrude. As she watched the children perform their nativity skit, breathed in the scent of pine boughs and candles, and sang the familiar carols, her own long-ago memories flooded in. Church attendance had been a spotty thing in her childhood, but for a stretch of several years, a neighboring family had taken her along to a Christmas craft workshop, where she'd enjoyed a few hours of contented concentration, making wreaths or pot holders or Styrofoam ornaments. Christmas music had poured out of speakers and people had been friendly and kind. For those short periods, she'd felt a part of a larger whole.

This seemed like the kind of church that would welcome a lonely child into their midst.

Maybe if she'd kept up her church attendance, she wouldn't have gone down the wrong path.

When the skit ended to enthusiastic applause, the children left, and Carson stood in the pulpit. He looked around as if meeting each individual's eyes. Was it her imagination, or did his gaze linger a little longer on her face?

"Did you know that Jesus was an outsider?" he began, and then continued on to preach a short but apt sermon, inviting everyone to recommit themselves to Christ, incarnated in the world, during this season.

He was a talented speaker, and Lily found herself thinking about the state of her own soul. She believed, read her Bible somewhat regularly, but she *did* feel like an outsider among religious folks. Her past had gone from isolated to wild, and while she'd straightened herself out overseas, with the help of a couple of Christian friends, she'd never found a church where she really belonged.

People in the congregation listened attentively, some smiling, others nodding. Carson seemed to be well respected.

And his kids obviously adored him.

So Pam's assessment of her husband was at least incomplete—she'd portrayed him as mean and abusive. She'd also said that he put on a good show, of course, and maybe that was what was happening tonight. But as the service ended and she watched Carson greet people by name and ask about their families, she couldn't detect even a note of insincerity.

It looked like he was going to be busy for a while, and the twins were still working on a craft in the Sunday school classroom. So Lily took a cup of hot apple cider from a smiling teenager and wandered off toward the small church library.

She didn't browse for long before the woman watching over the library struck up a conversation that ended in an invitation for Lily to come for Christmas dinner. Even though she turned it down, the offer lifted Lily's spirits. Then the clerk from the hardware store came over and started talking photography. Before she knew it, she was sitting in a small grouping of chairs, eating cookies and listening to a trio of women venting about how stressed they felt from Christmas preparations and expressing envy for her single, unencumbered state.

Yes, this was how church should be. Friendly and open and welcoming.

If she settled in a place like this, this was the type of church she'd want to attend.

"Lily." There was a touch on her shoulder, and she turned to see Carson's serious face. His interruption made the other three women exclaim about the time and get up to join the thinning crowd, collecting coats and children and heading out into the late-afternoon light.

Lily's heart thumped in a heavy rhythm as Carson sat down kitty-corner from her. She looked around the church lobby, desperate for a distraction, an excuse to escape. Why hadn't she used the church service as a time to figure out what she could say to this curious, grieving husband?

What could she say that wouldn't devastate him?

"When I heard your full name, I realized that you were Pam's roommate," he began. "That surprised me. Did you come to Esperanza Springs because of Pam? Is there anything you can tell me about her?"

Lily shook her head rapidly. "I didn't realize you all were here. At the ranch, I mean," she added, to keep from lying. "I'm just here to photograph the dogs for a project I'm finishing up. And to take your family pictures, remember? The gift from Penny." She was blathering.

And all of it was to deflect his interest away from her real purpose: to check on his daughters, for Pam.

His head tilted to one side, and there was a skeptical expression on his face. He opened his mouth to say something more.

"Pastor! There you are. I have a little gift for you

and your girls." A curvy woman with reddish hair thrust a container of cookies into Carson's hands.

"Thank you, Mariana." Carson's smile looked strained.

"I don't believe we've met." Mariana fixed Lily with an accusing glare.

"I'm sorry," Carson said. "Mariana, this is Lily, one of Pam's friends."

"Pleased to meet you." Mariana sounded anything but. "We all wanted to get to know Pam, but she was never around."

"I'm glad to meet you, too," Lily said in a weak response. She'd never thought about Pam's career from her hometown's point of view. It *was* odd that Pam had spent most of her leaves traveling, rather than being home with her family.

Mariana had just sat down when a teenage voice called from the doorway. "Mom! Let's go!"

"Kids." With a heavy sigh, Mariana stood, waved and walked toward the door.

Now the lobby area was almost completely empty, and parents were coming out from the back hallway with young children in hand. If Lily could only stall...

"Listen, we don't have much time," Carson said, "but I also know you won't be around long. That's why I'm really eager to talk with you about Pam. Do you know the circumstances of her last days?"

Lily blew out a sigh. "Didn't they contact you? Usually the army is good about—"

"Yes, they contacted me and gave me the official version," Carson interrupted. "But you and I both know that the official version isn't the whole story.

What was her state of mind, what had she been doing beforehand, that sort of thing."

Exactly what Lily didn't want to talk about, couldn't bear to talk about. "I think I hear your girls," she said desperately, standing up.

"Is there something I should know?" Carson stood, too, and stepped closer.

"No." He most definitely *shouldn't* know what had happened. It would only add to his unhappiness. "No, there's nothing you should know. I'll be outside." She spun and hurried toward the door.

Why had she done that? Now he would know there was something she wasn't saying. It would be so great to be a good liar, to be able to smile and tell Carson that Pam had spent her last moments thinking of him and her girls. That she'd been happy and content until the horrible accident had happened.

But Lily was a bad liar, and the pretty version was far from the truth.

She pushed open the door and walked out into a sunset world of cold and whirling snowflakes.

Almost an hour later, after a neck-tensing drive to the ranch in whiteout conditions, Carson gratefully pulled his truck into the driveway between Cabin Four and Cabin Five. He got out and came around to find Lily already opening the door for the girls.

"Yay! Snow!" Sunny called. "C'mon, Skye!"

But Skye was clinging to Lily's gloved hand. "Can you come in our cabin? We put out food for Santa every year."

Worry stabbed at Carson. Skye seemed to already be getting overly attached to Lily.

Lily smiled down at Skye. "That's such a nice offer, but I'd better not," she said without offering an excuse. "Run and see if you can catch a snowflake on your tongue!"

Distracted, Skye danced toward her sister, tongue out.

Carson handed Lily her package from the hardware store. "Let's finish our conversation later, or tomorrow," he said, by way of warning her that their talk wasn't over.

She'd obviously not wanted to discuss Pam, and possible reasons why were driving Carson crazy. Pam had been high-strung and intense, not without her problems and issues. Lily might know something about Pam's death, or her last days, that would shed some light.

Had she also known that Pam was pregnant again?

Even the thought of it stabbed at his heart. Carson had begged her not to go back into the army, to stay home instead. She could have easily gotten a discharge or at least a desk job. But she'd refused. She'd loved the excitement of being overseas. She'd said she wanted one last adventure before she really settled down.

The strong implication being *settled down with her boring old husband.*

But she'd promised to be careful and to tell her commanding officers about the pregnancy, and she'd assured him she wouldn't be assigned to any dangerous missions.

So how was it that she'd died from enemy fire?

The loss he'd faced had been double: his wife and his unborn child. To get over it, to move forward with his life, he needed more information, and the army's official materials hadn't satisfied him.

"Thanks for the ride," Lily said. She headed toward her cabin, then turned back. "Merry Christmas."

"Same to you." He watched her walk, straight-backed and lonely-looking, toward her cabin to spend the rest of Christmas Eve, and Christmas, alone.

He guessed people might feel sorry for him, too, but at least he had his girls. A true blessing.

"Daddy! Come here!" The twins were jumping up and down on the cabin's porch, and Carson hurried to them, concerned that even their slight weight would cause the old porch to cave in.

But when he got there, the porch was sturdy and intact, and the twins waved a large red envelope.

"Read it, Daddy, read it!" Sunny said.

He opened the envelope and read, in shaky handwriting: *You are cordially invited to a Christmas Eve dinner in Cabin 1. Banjo music included.*

He chuckled. He'd planned to serve the girls canned soup and grilled cheese tonight, waiting until tomorrow to attempt to cook the turkey and potatoes he'd bought, but a real, full dinner would be far preferable. And behind the cheerful wording of the invitation was the obvious: Long John wanted the company.

"What does it say?" Skye asked.

He knelt and read it to the girls, earning squeals of excitement.

"Let's put our things away first," he said, "and then we'll head down to see Mr. Long John."

"Let's go now!" Sunny held up the package containing the ornaments they'd bought at the hardware store.

"Because Mr. Long John doesn't have any decorations for his tree, and we can put ours on it."

"Good idea." There was no point in getting the girls out of their coats just to put them on again. He stowed the rock salt he'd bought on the cabin's porch and followed the girls through the snow to Long John's cabin.

As they climbed the porch steps, there was a rustling sound behind them, and Carson turned and saw Lily approaching, carrying a big shopping bag.

"Yay! He invited you, too!" Sunny jumped up and down.

Carson's heart picked up its pace. Not because of her slender figure and pretty, flushed cheeks, he told himself sternly. Only because he saw the possibility of having his talk with her sooner than he'd expected.

Long John opened the door, and his weathered face broke into a big smile. "What do you know, Rockette, we've got company!"

The dog lumbered to her feet, let out a deep "woof" and nudged at the twins, making them giggle.

Lily smiled down at the scene. "Dogs are such a gift. They make everyone happy."

"You folks didn't need to bring anything," Long John said as he ushered them into his cabin. "I mean this to be my treat, and a chance for you to relax. Come on, hang your coats right on that rack."

Carson turned to help the twins with their jackets and saw that Lily was already unzipping Skye's. He helped Sunny out of hers. Convenient. Two girls, two adults.

"We brought things to decorate your tree!" Sunny cried, twisting free of her jacket and hurtling over to the bag they'd brought. "See, look, there's orderments!"

"*Ornaments*, right, Daddy?" Skye asked.

"Why, they're right pretty," Long John interrupted with a wink at Carson. "But I would hate to use up the decorations you planned to put on your own tree."

"Go for it," Carson said, at the same time that Skye said, "It's okay." Both girls hurried over to Long John's waist-high, potted Norfolk Island pine.

"Thank you for inviting me," Lily was saying to Long John. She didn't hug him, but she clasped both of his hands.

"I'm just glad you all could come," the older man said, "because I've cooked up enough food for a battalion. I'd be hard-pressed to eat it all myself."

"I brought things to make cookies," Lily said. "If you'll let me mix up the batter and start them baking before dinner, the girls can decorate them afterward. Or take them home to decorate, if the party winds down."

"This party isn't winding down until midnight!" Long John said indignantly.

Lily lifted an eyebrow and tilted her head to one side, the corners of her mouth turning up. "You think you can outparty me? Game on."

She was obviously just joking, but Long John chuckled as he patted Lily's arm, and Carson's heart warmed. He hadn't been sure Lily really wanted to join in the gathering, but she was entering into the spirit of it, being kind to the girls and to Long John.

Long John led Lily to the kitchen area, showing her where things were and opening pots to stir them. A sweet-tart smell, ham baking, filled the air. The girls took turns placing ornaments on the little tree, for once not one-upping each other, but having fun together.

Unexpectedly, Carson's eyes prickled with tears.

This was what he'd wanted for his girls. A warm family Christmas. And if the family wasn't one of blood, well, that didn't matter. What mattered was the caring in their hearts. He let his eyes close, to keep the tears from spilling, but also to offer up a silent prayer of thanks.

Later in the evening, Lily wiped frosting from the twins' faces, then attempted to clean up the multiple splatters on the kitchen counter. In front of the fire, Long John plucked at his banjo while Carson strung lights on the little Christmas tree.

"Daddy! Mr. Long John! Come see our cookies!" Sunny crowed.

"They're soooooo beautiful," Skye added, admiring the two colorful platefuls.

Lily bit back a laugh. Piled high with frosting, plus sprinkles and colored sugar they'd found at Long John's friend's house next door, the lopsided cookies wouldn't be considered beautiful in any standard sense.

The twins' happy faces, though, made up for any imperfections in the cookies they'd decorated. And the fact that Lily had found a way to help these motherless girls—Pam's girls—have a little more Christmas joy opened a corner of her heart that had long ago closed down.

"Now ain't those the prettiest cookies ever," Long John said, leaning down to admire them. "Do I get to sample one?"

"Choose mine! Mine are on that plate!" Sunny begged.

"Mine are these," Skye said, pointing to the other plate.

"I think I'd like to try one of each," Long John said diplomatically, and a moment later Carson did the same.

"This is the best Christmas ever," Sunny said, and Skye nodded solemnly.

At that, Lily's good warm feelings drained away. This was most assuredly *not* the best Christmas the twins had ever experienced, nor Carson, either. Because Pam wasn't here. She looked uneasily at Carson and caught the stricken expression on his face.

"I don't think I'll make it until midnight after all," she said quickly. "I'm going to head back to my cabin. Thank you for your hospitality." She gave Long John a quick hug and then knelt and did the same for the girls.

Sunny yawned hugely and leaned into Carson's leg, while Skye ran to get Lily a cookie to eat later. Long John scooped ham and vegetables into a plastic container and insisted she take the leftovers along for Christmas dinner tomorrow.

"I'll walk you back," Carson said as she shrugged into her parka.

"No need. You stay with your girls."

"Then I'll watch from the porch to make sure you get there safely," he said, plucking his own parka from the hook.

She couldn't think of an argument against that, so she hurried out onto the porch. And gasped.

Snow blanketed everything—the trees, the fence, the cabins. There had to be six or eight inches.

"Whoa." Carson came to stand beside her, tapping

at his phone. "Snow's not letting up anytime soon," he said, holding up his weather app for her to see.

She blew out a sigh. "All the more reason for me to get settled inside. Thanks for driving me to town and…and for sharing your girls."

A small smile tugged at the corner of his mouth. "Thank you for entertaining them. They loved baking cookies." Suddenly, his gaze grew more intense. "They don't remember, but they did it with their mom, too."

"I know. She talked about it." Lily swallowed hard and started down the porch steps, picking her way carefully, but as quickly as possible.

"Lily," he said, and she turned. "Since it looks like we'll be snowed in, I'll stop over tomorrow to make sure you have everything you need," he said.

"Oh, you don't have to—"

"And," he interrupted, his voice decisive, "so we can finish our conversation about Pam."

Chapter Four

The next morning, Carson checked the cinnamon rolls in the oven, inhaling the rich, sweet smell, and then pulled out the hot chocolate mix. So the rolls were from a refrigerator tube and the cocoa was instant. The girls wouldn't care.

He paused to look out the cabin window. The sun was just starting to share its rosy light, illuminating the snowy mountains in the distance. He closed his eyes for a moment's thanks to the Creator: for the majesty outside, for the girls still sleeping in the loft upstairs and, most of all, for the Christ child who'd come into the world to save and bless them all.

He heard a rustle and a giggle upstairs and refocused on his cooking duties. He wanted to make this the best Christmas possible for his girls. Being here at the ranch, away from his computer and work tasks so he could focus on his girls, was a step in the right direction. And last night at Long John's house had been a good start to the festivities. Long John's funny songs and joke-telling had kept the girls laughing, and they'd loved playing with Rockette and decorating Long John's little tree.

And Lily! The way she'd helped the girls decorate cookies had given them such a good time. They'd talked about it, and her, until he'd tucked them into bed around midnight.

The pretty, cryptic woman had held Carson's attention, too. What motivated her to be so nice to the girls and to Long John?

And what did she know about Pam?

Her eyes had looked troubled both times Carson had brought her up. Why?

Was it something so bad she didn't want him to know, or had Pam made her promise secrecy?

Unfortunately, he had an idea of what the secret might be.

He heard another giggle and then some whispering. He poured water into the cups holding instant cocoa mix and pulled the cinnamon rolls out of the oven just in time, then snapped open the little container of sugary frosting and started slathering it on the hot rolls.

His mother's cinnamon rolls had been homemade, yeasty, buttery. He hadn't known how good he'd had it when he was a kid. But now, looking back, he could recognize that his parents had done their best to make Christmas festive and fun for him, even though, as the only child of only children, he hadn't had other kids with whom to share the holiday.

"Daddy!" The wooden ladder from the loft clattered alarmingly, and then the twins galloped across the cabin and flung their arms around him, nearly knocking him over in their enthusiasm.

"Merry Christmas!"

"Did Santa come?"

"Can we get in our stockings?"

"Let's open presents!"

He laughed, wiped his hands and knelt to hug them. "Merry Christmas, sweeties," he said. "I want you to eat a cinnamon roll first and we'll have a prayer and a little cocoa."

"Daddy!"

"And then, if you cooperate, we'll dig into the stockings."

They groaned but obediently sat down at the little table and held out their hands for a prayer. Carson thanked God for Christ, and their friends, and their family—quickly—and then helped them each to a cinnamon roll.

"These are good, Daddy!" Sunny said through a way-too-big bite.

Carson decided not to correct table manners on Christmas morning. He was just glad to get a little breakfast into the girls before the gift unwrapping madness began.

Of course, considering that they had candy galore in their stockings, he probably should have fixed something without quite so much sugar for breakfast.

But it was Christmas. He took another cinnamon roll himself. He'd work it off shoveling snow later today.

After the girls dumped out their stockings and gleefully examined all the candy and little windup toys and tiny bottles of scented shampoo and lotion and hand sanitizer, it was time for presents.

"Do we *have* to take turns?" Sunny asked.

"We always take turns!" Skye frowned at her sister. "And I think it's *my* turn to go first."

Carson grabbed a candy and put both hands behind his back. "Whoever guesses which hand has a peppermint in it goes first." After Skye guessed correctly, he averted Sunny's fuss by picking out two identical packages. "She'll go first *after* you both open these at the same time."

They ripped eagerly into the gifts and then raved over the pretty, fancily dressed dolls. They'd stretched Carson's budget, but he hadn't been able to resist after seeing the twins' longing faces when they'd shopped in Colorado Springs earlier this month.

While they examined each feature of the dolls and compared their outfits, Carson picked up an ornament one of the girls had knocked off the tree. When he saw which one it was, his heart twisted a little. It was a plastic ball made from a photo: him, Pam, and the girls as babies, all dressed up for Christmas.

He missed that family feeling. Missed the Pam of those days, when she'd been in love with being a mom. In love with him, at least a little bit.

Before she'd gotten restless with the whole package.

Maybe someday he'd be over the feelings of inadequacy and ready to move forward, find a new mom for his girls. Because no matter how happy they seemed now, rummaging under the tree for the next gift, he knew they needed a woman's influence and warmth.

So did he, if the truth be told.

"Open yours, Daddy!" Sunny cried as she handed him a clumsily wrapped gift.

"No, mine!" Skye held out a similar package, but then her face grew thoughtful, and she pulled it back.

"You can open hers first," she said, "since I get to open my package first."

"Nice, honey."

"I'm nice, too!" Sunny looked indignant. "I didn't fuss about her getting to open her gift first!"

Yes, Carson could use a partner just to help him handle the mathematics of making sure two little girls got equal time, gifts and love.

He ripped open the tube-shaped package and unrolled a cloth banner, a felt reindeer head with handprints for antlers. "I made it, Daddy," Sunny explained, fitting her hands over the handprints. "Those are my hands. And our teacher said the parents would be happy because our hands would never be the same size again."

"They're gonna grow much bigger," Skye explained. "Here, open mine."

He did, then exclaimed over the slightly neater reindeer Skye had produced, watched her show him how the antler-handprints fit her hands.

"Look on the back, look on the back!" They said it in unison, laughed and fist-bumped each other.

Carson turned both banners over and read the poem out loud.

"This year my hand is little,
But one day, when I'm tall,
This reindeer will remind you
Of the time when I was small."

His throat tightened, and he reached out to hug his daughters to him, one in each arm. "Thank you for the reindeer banners," he managed to choke out. "They're the best gifts I've ever gotten."

It was true. And he needed to remember to embrace this moment, not focus on the past or the future. This Christmas, at Redemption Ranch when the girls were six, would never happen again. One day, he'd look back and long for the sticky kisses and chocolaty handprints and excited bouncing of his twins, who were growing up at a way-too-rapid pace.

He cleared his throat. "Two more gifts for each of you," he said. "Skye, you first."

So Skye ripped into her art set. And then Sunny squealed over her remote-control car. And they both expressed dutiful enthusiasm for their third packages, containing warm winter outfits. It wasn't the extravagant set of gifts some kids got, he knew, but he'd done what he could, within his budget.

Besides, he liked to keep the focus on the real meaning of Christmas.

He stood to get a garbage bag for the wrapping paper scattered all over the floor and realized both twins were looking at him expectantly. "Go ahead," he said, "you play with your new toys. I'll clean up."

"Where is it?" Sunny asked.

"Where's what?"

"The puppy!" they both yelled.

He looked at them, confused. "What puppy?"

"He's joking!" They both hurled themselves at him, tugging his hands. "Daddy, stop joking! Where is it?"

He was getting a really bad feeling. He sank to his knees on the ground, still grasping their hands. "Hold on a minute," he said. "There's not a puppy."

Skye was the first one to realize he was serious. He could tell, because her eyes welled up with tears.

Sunny glanced at her twin, read the expression on her face and started beating her fist against Carson's chest. "There *is* a puppy! There *is*!"

"No, there isn't." He caught Sunny's fist in his hand as a heavy sensation settled around his heart. "No hitting. I don't know where you got the idea you were getting a puppy, but it's not true."

Skye turned to Sunny, hands on hips. "You *said*."

"Miss *Lily* said. And Krissy Morgan's getting a puppy, and her daddy isn't even very nice, so I thought—"

Lily had told them they were getting a puppy?

"Our daddy isn't nice, either," Skye stated. Then she sank to her knees and buried her face in her hands.

"We wanted a puppy," Sunny said, big tears rolling down her face. "We really wanted a puppy."

Carson pulled them both into his arms, his chest aching. "Sometimes we don't get everything we want," he said, trying to soothe them even as the words rang hollow in his own ears. Looking over their heads to the candy wrappers scattered across the floor, he realized that the crash from their sugar high wasn't helping things.

You're the worst father ever.

Pam's words, yelled in anger and quickly retracted, still rang in his ears. He looked at the ceiling. Right now, his angry wife seemed just about right.

Which didn't mean he could lash out or give up. He was the grown-up. "Look," he said, "I'm going to go make us some eggs. Sunny, you can come help me while Skye washes her face, and then you can trade places. After we've had some real breakfast, we'll play a board game or build a snowman."

He went into the kitchen, Sunny trailing mournfully after him. As he got out eggs and broke them and then let her beat them with a fork, he berated himself. He should have realized they'd be hoping for a puppy. It was what they'd been talking about for weeks.

He should have sat them down and talked seriously about what was realistic, rather than just saying "no" and letting his refusal be laughed off.

"I'm sorry you were disappointed, kiddo," he said when Sunny handed him the bowl of beaten eggs. "What are you going to play with first, your doll or your car?"

"I don't care," she said sulkily, but then she added, "Probably the car."

He set butter melting in a pan and then told Sunny to go wash her face. "Send Skye in to help with the toast while you get cleaned up," he said, realizing belatedly that he should have had her wash her hands *before* cooking. Oh, well. Priorities.

A moment later, Sunny came back into the kitchen. "Hey, Daddy."

"Yeah." He turned down the heat and poured the eggs into the frying pan.

"I can't find Skye," she said.

Lily headed down the road that cut across the ranch. It was the only spot where the walking was easy, since some Good Samaritan had already been through to plow the foot and a half of snow that had fallen last night.

She shouldn't have even glanced in the window at

Carson and the girls, but their cabin had been lit up like a theater. A theater showing the perfect family Christmas. The girls ripping open their packages, and Carson's hug when he'd opened his; lots of smiles and laughter. The way Christmas should be but rarely was, especially in her experience.

Then again, Carson and the twins didn't have things perfect: missing from the picture was Pam.

And her absence was Lily's fault.

She pushed away that thought and tramped along, her ancient boots crunching on the packed snow and ice. If she stayed here, she'd need to get some new ones.

But what was she thinking? She wasn't going to stay here.

She looked out across the wide-open spaces. The air was so clear that the distant mountains seemed to be cut out of cardboard, so crisp and distinct were the edges of them against the blue sky. The snow sparkled bright, making her wish she'd remembered to bring her sunglasses along. But who would have thought you'd need sunglasses in the dead of winter? Lily associated them with hot Phoenix sun.

Her breath made clouds as she debated whether to go back and get her sunglasses. It would be more comfortable. And why not? She had nothing else to do on Christmas Day.

No self-pity, she warned herself as she turned to climb back up the road. *Plenty of people have things a lot worse than this.* She'd get her sunglasses and take a nice long walk, then go inside and eat the leftovers Long John had pressed on her last night. In the afternoon, she'd get busy on her project of photographing the dogs. It would be good for them to get the extra attention, and good for her to get a big chunk of her project done. Unlike people, dogs weren't busy with family activities on Christmas—at least shelter dogs weren't.

When she got closer to her cabin, she heard a sound, like a kitten crying. She walked faster, craning to see.

A flash of bright pajamas. One of the twins, huddled by her front door. What in the world?

She ran the rest of the way to her cabin and picked up the little girl. "Honey, you're not wearing your coat! Let's get you back home."

"Can I come in your house?" she asked, sniffling.

"For a minute." It wasn't a bad idea to get a blanket to wrap around the child before carrying her back over to Carson's house. "You're Skye, right?"

The little girl nodded and sat obediently on the couch while Lily found a fleecy blanket to wrap around her. "Does your father know you're here?"

She shrugged.

"He must be worried sick about you. Let's get you back over there." She picked the child up and carried her out onto the porch.

"I wanted a dog so bad." Skye buried her head in Lily's shoulder. "But we didn't get one."

Lily's heart ached as the little girl clung to her. Christmas disappointment was the worst when you were a kid.

"I thought maybe *you* got us a dog," Skye said as Lily shifted her to her opposite side to shut the front door. Man, six-year-olds were heavy.

"You thought what?" she asked absently.

"I thought maybe you got us a dog, because you said…"

Lily closed the cabin door, shifted Skye into a more secure position and started down the steps, careful of her footing. "What did I say?"

"You said, dogs are gifts. And we thought that meant…"

"Oh, honey, no!" Lily's stomach twisted and she hugged the child closer, still walking toward the cabin next door. "I meant dogs are a gift from God, such wonderful companions, but I didn't mean that you'd get a dog as a Christmas present." Trust a child to be literal that way.

Skye buried her head in Lily's shoulder and shook with a couple more sobs as Lily approached the other cabin.

The door burst open, and Carson came out, bundled up, with Sunny right behind him. "Skye!" he cried when he saw her and Lily. He rushed forward and took her from Lily's arms. "Where did you go? I was worried!"

"She was on my porch when I got back from a walk," Lily said. "I wrapped a blanket around her, but she's still shivering." Like she could tell this experienced parent anything about his daughter.

He was already turning back to his cabin. "Let's get you inside."

Lily stopped and watched the trio head into Carson's cabin. Her work was done. She'd get her sunglasses and go back to her walk, which now felt even more solitary.

Had she really made the girls think they'd get a puppy? How awful. Chalk it up to her inexperience with kids. Head down, she turned back toward her cabin.

"Lily!" It was Carson's voice.

She pretended she didn't hear. Cowardly, but she didn't want to be berated for her mistake.

There was the sound of crunching footsteps, and then a small, cold hand clasped hers.

"Daddy wants you to come over to our house," Sunny said, smiling up at Lily. "Will you?"

"Oh, honey, I…"

"He wants to say thank you. And you could look at our new toys. Please?"

No human with a heart could turn down the childish plea in those round eyes, that sweet face. "I'll come over for a few minutes," she said. She'd pay a little visit, confess to Carson about her unfortunate choice of dog-related words yesterday, and ooh and aah over the girls' toys. And then she'd get on with her hike.

Inside the little cabin, Carson sat in a big chair next to the fire, holding Skye. He smiled up at Lily, his eyes crinkling at the corners. "Thank you for helping Skye," he said. "Won't you stay and have some scrambled eggs with us?"

"Oh, I couldn't, I—"

"Have too much else to do?" His eyes were too observant.

"Maybe I do," she snapped, and then felt awful for it. "I'm sorry. I… Sunny mentioned wanting me to see their new toys, but I don't want to intrude on your family Christmas."

"Look at my doll!" Sunny thrust it into Lily's arms. "Come on, help me change her clothes. I got three outfits for her, in the box. Skye's doll only has two, but one of them is a fancy ball gown, so it costed more."

"She's beautiful," Lily said, running her fingers

over the doll's furry snow jacket. "Look, her eyes are the same color as yours. And they open and close."

"And her hair's pretty. I'm going to try to keep it pretty, cuz my other doll's hair is a mess. I washed it with soap, and I wasn't supposed to."

As Sunny prattled on, Lily slipped out of her coat and helped the little girl change her doll's clothes while covertly observing Carson. He was talking seriously to Skye, and she could catch a few of the quiet words. "Careful" and "no leaving without me" and "I was worried."

No yelling, hitting, even scolding. Just a caring, concerned parent.

Pam had been wrong about her husband. How had she been so wrong?

Soon Skye wiggled off her father's lap and came over to join them. Lily glanced back and saw Carson head for the kitchen area. So she looked at Skye's doll and helped with her wardrobe change as well, and pretty soon they were involved in a game of pretend.

"I want a dog!" Sunny made her doll say, poking at the other doll with a stiff, outstretched arm.

"No!" Skye batted the doll's hand away with her own doll. "You can't have one."

"Why not?"

"Because you don't help your daddy enough, and he's busy, busy, busy." The words were spoken by Skye in an adult inflection that made Lily smile a little.

"I'll help more," Sunny's doll said. "I'll clean the floor and take out the garbage and cook—"

"You're not allowed to cook," Skye's doll said, pointing her plastic arm at Sunny. "You're too little."

"*You're* too little!" Sunny's doll cried.

Lily put a finger to her lips. "Quiet dolls get more attention," she said, having no idea where it came from. "And any-age doll can pretend cook, right?"

Both girls frowned thoughtfully. "Then," Skye said, "can we pretend get a dog?"

Oh, boy. Lily didn't want to say the wrong thing again, but both pairs of eyes looked at her expectantly. Amazing how little kids thought adults knew everything.

"Your dolls might be able to get a pretend dog," she said carefully, "as long as you know it's not real. And as long as you don't use it to torture your daddy."

"What's torture?" Skye asked, just as Carson came over from the kitchen area.

Lily looked up at him, afraid she'd really said something wrong, but he just lifted an eyebrow.

"I was exaggerating," she said to the girls. "I only meant that you shouldn't use your pretend dog to bother your father and beg for a real one all the time." She leaned forward and beckoned the little girls closer and whispered, "Bugging him probably won't work at all, but if he sees you play nicely with your pretend dog and do your chores, maybe he'll change his mind."

"Yay!" Both twins jumped up and danced around. "We're getting a dog, we're getting a dog."

"No, I didn't mean—" Lily looked desperately at Carson, whose forehead was wrinkled, the corners of his mouth turned down. "Girls, that—what you're doing right now—that's bugging him and torturing him." She blew out a breath and looked at Carson. "I'm just digging myself in deeper and deeper. I'd better leave while you're still speaking to me."

He chuckled ruefully. "You may as well stay. I have

way too much cheesy scrambled eggs for the three of us. And toast, and fruit."

The smells coming out of the kitchen made Lily's stomach growl audibly. "If you're sure."

"I'm sure," he said, giving her a half smile. "Just, please, let's change the subject from dogs, okay?"

"Of course. I'm sorry. I think something I said yesterday was what gave them the impression that they were getting a dog. I'm really sorry. I said 'dogs are a gift' and…"

"And they heard what they want to hear. Welcome to six-year-olds." He clapped his hands. "Girls, I want you to wash your hands and then come to the table. You can show Miss Lily where to wash her hands, too. We all need a little breakfast before we decide what to do with the rest of our day."

After they'd stuffed themselves on breakfast food—including cinnamon rolls left over from their earlier meal—Carson cleared his throat to get the girls' attention. "Let's everyone say one thing they'd like to do on Christmas," he suggested, and Lily nodded approval of his parenting skills. In her own family, no such open communication had happened; the adults had done what they wanted—usually involving drinking—and Lily had taken refuge in drawing and books and, one year, the camera Aunt Penny had sent her in the mail. That wonderful gift had impacted her career decisions both in the military and after.

"I want to go sledding!" Skye cried.

"I want to build a snowman," Sunny said.

They all looked expectantly at Lily. "Ummmmm… I want to go take pictures of the dogs in the barn, for my school project."

"No more dogs," Carson groaned.

"I'm sorry!"

Lily clapped her hands to her mouth as the girls chanted, "The dogs, the dogs!"

She'd done it again. She was causing more trouble in this family.

And this was just superficial stuff compared to what she'd done to Pam, the girls' mother, Carson's beloved wife. "Hey, listen, I'd better go," she said, and stood. "Thank you for the breakfast."

"Don't go, Miss Lily!" Skye said.

She high-fived each of the girls. "I've got a hike to take, and you've got a snowman to build!" She gave Carson a quick wave, grabbed her coat and headed outside.

She needed to escape before she made more trouble for Carson. And before he roped her into talking about Pam again.

Chapter Five

"Wait!" Carson stood and followed Lily, stopping at the cabin door.

Still on the porch, she turned. She looked over her shoulder, biting her lip, her blue coat bright against a background of diamond-crusted snow.

"I didn't mean you should leave. Visiting the dogs isn't a bad idea." He couldn't believe he was saying that.

But he didn't want Lily to go, and when he examined his reasons, he wasn't entirely sure what they were.

One of them, he reminded himself firmly, was finding out more about Pam's death. Because Carson needed to move on. As the girls got older, he was realizing just how much they needed a mother's touch; witness their clingy behavior toward Lily. Their concerns and issues were getting more complicated, too. He needed a partner in parenting.

The undeniable tug he felt toward Lily reminded him he might need a partner's love and companionship for himself, too.

"I want to go visit Long John and see how his Christmas is going," Carson said, directing the comment to both Lily and the girls, who were now pressing against his sides. "And then we'll do a little sledding and snowman-building, and then we'll see." He reached out toward Lily, an automatic welcoming gesture.

At least, he thought that was all it was.

She looked at his hand and then at him, and a flush rose to her cheeks.

What did *that* mean?

"We'd be honored if you'd stay and spend more time with us," he said.

The girls pushed their way past him and out the door, tugging at Lily with their surely very sticky hands. "Stay! Play with us today!"

Yes. They needed for Carson to find them a mother figure, and soon. They were attaching themselves to Lily way too much, too soon, and he shouldn't be encouraging it.

After he'd found out what he wanted to know— and tried to offer her some counseling and support, as he'd promised Penny he would—he'd create some natural distance.

And then this Christmastime at the ranch would be over, and they'd go their separate ways.

He shook that thought away as Lily looked searchingly at him. "If you're sure, I'll visit with you for a little while," she said, her voice hesitating. Obviously, she was uncertain of her welcome.

Or was she hiding something? What did she know about Pam?

Thoughts of his wife's flirtatious behavior with

other men crowded in, even as he tried to push them away. Had Pam been headed for an assignation with a lover when she'd blundered into enemy fire? Did Lily know something about it, and was she just too kind to tell him?

"Come on, girls—coats and boots and hats and mittens before we can play in the snow," he said, and the flurry of getting them and himself ready, of pulling saucer sleds out of the truck and finding a suitably safe hill for sledding, helped to clear his thoughts.

The safest hill they found sloped down from Long John's cabin, so Lily and Carson stood at the top and watched the girls race each other on their plastic sleds, squealing. Long John came out on his little back deck and waved, but declined their invitation to come down.

"I'm taking it easy today," he said. Code for his Parkinson's acting up, Carson suspected.

"Are you sure?" Lily smiled at the older man. "It's a beautiful day. We can come up and help you."

"No, thanks. I'm just going to stay inside and watch my birds." Long John gestured toward the seed-and-peanut-butter pinecones he'd hung all around the porch. Nuthatches and warblers darted and flew around them.

Long John waved and went inside. A moment later he appeared in his chair by the window, where he could watch his birds and the girls, too.

"He's good at making a life for himself," Lily said thoughtfully. "We could all learn something from him."

"That's true." They walked over a few feet to where there was a big rock to perch on. A couple of ponderosa pines loomed behind them, and Lily looked up. "They're so beautiful," she said. "I love the green against the blue sky and the snow."

A bit of nature lore emerged from somewhere in the back of his brain. "Smell the trunk of the tree," he urged her.

"*Smell* it?"

He nodded, and gamely she walked up to the trunk and sniffed. Her face lit up. "Butterscotch?"

"Or vanilla. It's the only tree that smells like cookies."

"That's so cool!" Her cheeks were pink and just for a minute she looked carefree and delighted.

Carson couldn't take his eyes off her.

She flushed and looked away. Then she frowned up at Carson. "Hey, I'm sorry I contributed to that mess with the dogs. I shouldn't have even mentioned dogs to the girls. I hated to see them so upset."

"They've rebounded quickly." Carson gestured toward the twins as they reached the top of the little slope, tugging their plastic sleds, and then plopped down together to slide down the hill again. "Don't blame yourself. I feel bad about not getting them the present they really wanted, but the truth is, I'm hard-pressed to manage our home life already. Taking care of a puppy is beyond me."

"You seem like you're doing a great job."

"Thank you." He hesitated as a natural way into a difficult conversation came to him. "Did Pam say anything to you about how I was as a father?"

Lily looked at him quickly and then looked away. "Not really," she said, her voice uneasy.

"How well did you and Pam know each other?" he pressed. "From what she said, you were pretty close."

In fact, he'd gotten a completely different impression of Lily from Pam than how she was now. Pam had made it sound like she was a drinker and partier, wilder even than Pam herself.

The woman beside him didn't match that description at all. Could she have changed that much? Or had Pam been wrong?

"Miss Lily! Come sledding!"

"Okay!" Lily slogged through the snow toward them without a glance back at Carson, which left him wondering: What would have been her answer to his question?

Later that afternoon, Lily sat wrapped in a snug fleece blanket in a comfortable chair in her cabin, trying to read a Christmas book.

The picture on the cover, a snow-covered Victorian home all decorated for Christmas, matched the sweet story, and normally she'd have been swept away. But her eyes kept drifting to the window and the scene outside.

Carson and the twins were building a snowman, laughing and shouting. They'd gotten one giant ball on top of the other to form the snowman's body and now were rolling a smaller ball for the head.

She watched Carson kneel to help the girls pat more snow into place. He was a good man, a good dad. When he'd asked her how well she and Pam had known each other, what Pam had said about him, she hadn't wanted to tell him. Still didn't.

It was hard to understand why Pam had misled her so badly. Why had Pam wanted her to think she had an abusive husband? Was it possible that Carson used to be that way? After all, Lily herself had done a 180-degree turnaround in the past few years. Maybe Carson had, too.

But watching his gentleness with his girls, noticing the way he interacted with Long John and his parishioners, it was simply impossible to imagine that he'd ever been the bully of Pam's vivid stories.

Maybe she *should* tell him the truth. Was it worse to mislead someone, or to knowingly hurt them?

This morning, the opportunity to ride a sleigh down the hill with the girls had come as a welcome interruption. When Carson had approached her again, she'd pleaded cold and work and gone inside.

But it bothered her. She and Pam had started out so close. Notorious for being the most party-happy females on the base, they'd spent a lot of time together in all sorts of conditions.

Which made the way things had ended even worse.

And if there had been a sense of betrayal between Lily and Pam, how much worse would Pam's final actions feel to Carson, her husband?

Lily should have found a better way to handle the whole situation. Should have sat down in a friendly way with Carson and told him, "Look, here's what Pam said, here's what happened."

Lily couldn't figure out a way to do that without hurting Carson in the process. And a selfish part of her didn't want to admit her own role, to destroy forever the warm way he'd looked at her.

A knock on the door, followed by a high, piping "Miss Lily!" pulled her out of her low thoughts.

She hurried over and opened the door, and the sight

of Sunny and Skye made her smile. "Hi, girls! How's the snowman coming along?"

"He's getting real big!" Skye said, pointing.

"But we need help," Sunny added. "Do you have a carrot for his nose?"

She looked over their heads to where Carson was shoveling, but he didn't glance their way. Did he know the girls were here? Had he encouraged them to come?

"I do have a carrot," she said slowly. "Come on inside and I'll get it for you."

They came inside but stayed on the mat by the door. "Your cabin is a lot like ours," Skye said. "And you like to read, too, just like Daddy!"

"Does your dad read to you?" she asked as she pulled a couple of carrots from her refrigerator.

"Uh-huh. Right now, he's reading us a Christmas book called *The Story of Holly and Ivy*, about a little girl who doesn't have a family."

"It's sad," Skye said, "but Daddy promised us it will have a happy ending. Will you come out and help us finish our snowman?"

Lily made a pretense of washing the carrots while she pondered. She wasn't exactly enjoying her solitary time in the cabin, and she'd been watching the progress of the snowman with interest. It was beautiful and sunny out, and she'd love to get a little more fresh air.

And company, she realized. Seeing Carson and his girls made her aware of the family she didn't have.

But she didn't need to get any more involved with them. Didn't need to hear any more of Carson's questions, nor struggle more to conceal the truth.

She turned toward the girls, and the sight of the two

eager faces swayed her resolve to stay inside. "Here you go," she said.

"Won't you come?"

Inspiration hit. "I'll bring my camera," she said, "and take some of the family photos I'm supposed to do. We'll do some today and some tomorrow. That way, we'll have different lights and clothes."

And she'd have a barrier between herself and Carson. The camera could be a friend that way, giving her something to do and allowing the right amount of distance from people.

She pulled on her coat and mittens and boots and followed the girls outside, inhaling the fresh, cold air. Notes of pine and spruce added to the holiday feeling, and sun sparkled off the snow.

You couldn't doubt the existence of God when you saw His amazing handiwork.

She picked up Skye and let her poke the carrot in for the nose, noticing that she had a tiny mole on her cheek. Then she lifted up Sunny to put in the chocolate-cookie eyes Carson had brought out. This close, she could see that Sunny had a tiny scar in her hairline.

So they weren't identical, and Lily felt satisfied knowing that she could tell them apart, even if they were sleeping.

Although, why would that be of interest to her? It wasn't as if she were going to be involved with this family after the holidays.

"So they talked you into coming out again?" Carson's deep, friendly voice behind her danced along her nerve endings.

She held up her camera like a shield. "I thought I'd

get some of the family photos done today," she said, "if that's okay with you."

"We're not exactly dressed up for the occasion," he said. "I ought to at least comb their hair. And mine," he added, forking fingers through his already mussed hair.

Lily shook her head. "You're all rosy and active and happy. These will be great pictures. We'll do dress-up clothes by the fireplace tomorrow."

"If you're sure." He looked at her just a little longer than was necessary.

She broke her gaze away and studied her camera, making small adjustments, taking deep breaths. It must be the season that was giving her these odd feelings about Carson. She wasn't one to get all fluttery around a man.

Carson tied a scarf around the snowman's neck and then lifted the girls, one in each arm, to place his hat. Lily snapped photo after photo as they laughed and adjusted it. She could tell already that these would be a delight, much more appealing than anything posed.

"Come here, Miss Lily, let Daddy take your picture with us!"

Lily glanced at Carson to see him looking at her with his head cocked to one side. Was he thinking that it was inappropriate for her, a stranger, to be in a photo with his girls? Or that he'd like to see it?

He held out his phone. "I'll just use this," he said. "Your camera looks too high-tech for me."

So she knelt beside the snowman, one girl on either side of her, and let him take pictures. As the girls laughed and mugged for the camera, she couldn't help joining in. They were irresistible, these two sweethearts.

"Did you ever make snow angels?" she asked them.

They both frowned and shook their heads. "Show us how!"

So she lay down and moved her arms and legs, showing them how to make angels in the snow. Then she helped each of them do the same.

"I'm going to call my angel Miss Lily!" Sunny said.,

Skye looked thoughtful. "I'm going to call mine Mommy," she said, "because our mommy would think they were pretty. Only, she can't see them, because she's in heaven."

The words made Lily's breath catch, and she glanced at Carson. His mouth had twisted to one side as he studied her and the girls.

Grief and shame pushed at her, but she didn't get to wallow in her feelings, not when there were little girls to watch out for. She knelt and gave Skye a quick hug, then reached to have Sunny join in. "Your mommy just might be smiling from heaven to see your snow angels," she said, "and that's nice you're naming yours after her. But it's sweet you named one after me, too."

Both girls clung on a little longer than she expected and she felt her chest tighten. Such dear children. They shouldn't have lost their mother. *Oh, Pam, why did you do what you did? How could you leave your girls motherless?*

"Why don't you make two more snowmen? Little ones, twin kids," Carson suggested.

"Yeah!"

"Will you help?"

"I wonder if you can figure out how to do it yourself, now that you've had some practice?" Carson asked.

Hmm. Good parenting, or a desire to talk to Lily apart from the girls, especially now that Pam had figured so prominently in the conversation?

She supposed it was inevitable, so she brushed snow off her jacket and went to stand beside him. For a moment, they watched the girls argue about how to get started, and then Lily heard a sharp tapping, like a rapid drum. "What's that?" she asked.

He looked around and then pointed. "There," he said.

"Where?"

He came closer so she could look along his arm to his pointing finger, and she caught a whiff of his spicy aftershave. "See the bird?" he asked.

She saw it then, a small black, gray and white creature with a bright red spot on its head.

It seemed to notice them, for it stopped drilling, cocked its head and offered a quiet *pik-pik-pik-pik*.

"Downy woodpecker," he volunteered.

She studied him. "How come a pastor knows so much about the outdoors?" she asked.

He laughed, a little self-consciously. "I was an only child. Spent a lot of time outdoors with my grandpa, and he taught me the names of the trees and the birds." He laughed. "Pretty geeky, huh?"

"I think it's cool," she said. "When I was a kid, Aunt Penny sent me this deck of card-like things, birds of the Plains. I went all over my street and the fields nearby, trying to identify stuff."

He smiled, started to say something, shook his head.

"What?"

"We have some things in common. Things Pam and I didn't."

She didn't answer, afraid to walk onto that dangerous ground.

"You know," he said as the girls worked together on twin snowmen, "Pam made some mistakes. I know that."

She held her breath. What did he mean?

"You wouldn't be hurting her memory if you told me she had a boyfriend, and that somehow contributed to her getting shot."

She stared at him.

"I wasn't what she wanted. She told me. I wasn't exciting enough for her."

Lily blew out a breath. On the one hand, she knew what Carson was talking about. Pam had been a seeker, never satisfied with what she had, always wanting more.

But Carson was such an amazing man. How would any woman married to him want someone else?

Yes, Pam had been a flirt, and it had made Lily uncomfortable because Pam was married. But she'd never taken it far, and she'd laughed when Lily had questioned her actions. "I'm married, not dead!" she would say.

It had bothered Lily even more toward the end of Pam's time. When Pam had been drifting further and further away from Lily, when their lives had gone such different directions.

Once Lily had started studying the Bible, she'd realized that sins of thought and feeling counted, just like sins of action.

Raising those ideas with Pam, though, had been the beginning of the end of their friendship.

Carson was looking at her with calm expectation. How could a husband be that calm about the notion that his wife might have cheated on him?

"I mean, look at today," he said. "My girls wanted a puppy, and did I get them one? No. Because I'm boring and no fun, just like Pam said."

"Not true," she said firmly. "You know what you can handle and what's right for your family." She hesitated, wondering how much to say. But at least she could reassure him on one score. "She didn't have a boyfriend, Carson. If she had, she would've told me."

"I just keep trying to understand it," he said. "She wasn't supposed to be in the line of fire. And you knew... Did you know? She was expecting a baby."

"What?" She stared at him, his words echoing crazily in her ears.

Pam had been expecting a baby?

Expecting a baby.

A new wave of guilt washed over her, stealing her breath. By not saving Pam, Lily had deprived this family of a precious new member.

She knew, as a Christian, she was forgiven. *But for this, Lord? How can I be forgiven for this?*

"You didn't know?"

She shook her head. That made everything so much worse. "Look," she said desperately, "I'm so sorry. Sorry for your loss." She blew out a breath. She was going to lose it here. "It's been great to hang out with you guys, but I'm getting cold, and you need to spend time as a family. Take care, Carson." She gave him a little wave and headed off toward her cabin.

* * *

After his conversation with Lily—and her abrupt departure—Carson felt like the girls needed some quiet time. And Carson needed some advice on how to get the truth out of Lily. You and Rockette up for a visit? he texted Long John.

Come on over, was the reply.

Moments later, the girls were settled in front of a Christmas movie with the ever-patient Rockette while Long John and Carson, bundled up, examined the splintered porch.

They talked beams and nails and braces for a few minutes, and then Carson dived in. "What would you do if you wanted to know something and you knew somebody knew about it, and they wouldn't tell you?"

"Sounds like a puzzle." Long John's forehead wrinkled as he studied Carson. "Is this about Lily?"

How had the older man guessed so quickly? He nodded. "Uh-huh."

"I'd ask myself why. What could that person stand to lose?"

Carson shook his head. "I can't imagine. I've told her I understand that Pam was…or rather, that she wasn't…" He bit off the sentence.

Compassion spread over Long John's face. "I'd also ask myself," he said, "if I really wanted to know whatever truth that person was hiding."

Did he? "Yes," Carson said, "I think I do. I need to know so I can move on."

Long John picked up a handful of nails and began to sort them by size. "You sure you're not the one running away?" he asked. "If you've made this a barrier to getting involved with anyone else, well…" He didn't look at Carson but laid the nails down in a line, neat despite the Parkinson's tremor in his hands.

"I just…" Carson started pulling the rotting board from the porch, using the claw of the hammer. "If you've been married and it didn't go well, you ought to take a look at what happened. Especially when there are two little ones involved in any mistakes you might make."

"True enough," Long John said.

They were silent for a couple of minutes, Long John handing him nails as he moved down the new board, hammering. Then the older man said, "Sometimes, you have to turn to the Lord. Ever think about that?"

The words hit Carson like a hammer bigger than the one he held in his hand. "You shouldn't have to tell me that. Some preacher I am." He ought to be counseling Long John, not the other way around.

"Sometimes the doctor needs a doctor," Long John said. "You're young. Maybe too young to realize that moving on from what's hurt you in the past isn't always a matter of finding out every detail."

"But I want to know." Carson pounded in a nail with punishing force. And then another one. And then he glanced up to see Long John watching him steadily.

I'm angry, he realized. *But at whom?*

The sound of a car engine and tires crunching on snow were a welcome distraction. A big SUV pulled to a halt and one of his parishioners, Minnie Patton, climbed out.

Carson's heart sank a little, but he overcame it quickly. "Hello, Minnie," he called.

"The last thing I need is a visit from General Patton," Long John muttered beside him.

Carson swallowed a smile. He knew a number of church members called Minnie "The General," and it wasn't only because of her surname.

"I heard you were up here alone," Minnie said to Long John as she opened the back door of the SUV.

"He's not alone, Minnie," said a voice from the passenger seat. Beatrice, Minnie's younger sister, was a sweet woman who rarely got a word in edgewise.

Minnie pulled a large casserole dish from the back seat. "You shouldn't be out here in the cold," she scolded as she approached Long John.

"And Merry Christmas to you, Minnie," Long John said with a hint of sarcasm in his voice. "I'm going to say hello to your sister." His glance at Carson was eloquent: *save me.*

Carson watched as Long John greeted Beatrice, who lowered the window with a smile. Even from here, Carson could see the scarf that covered Beatrice's bald head, her pale, thin face. Chemo had been hard on her, and not the least of it was that she'd had to move in with Minnie.

As she looked up at Long John, though, Beatrice's eyes sparkled, and her thin face curved into a smile.

Carson shoved down a sigh as General Patton—Minnie—approached. "Merry Christmas," he said, shaking her hand.

"It would be merrier if you were down in town instead of up here vacationing like a man of leisure," she said. "What if someone in your congregation falls ill?"

The ones who need love the most are the hardest to love. "If someone from the church has a problem, I'll come down to town, of course. Let me help you with that casserole."

"I'll take it inside," she said, turning to block him from taking it from her. She was obviously planning to go in the house. Which presented its own set of problems, because the girls very distinctly didn't like Miss Minnie. Carson couldn't blame them; no one liked being called "poor little motherless things."

"Long John," Carson called, still standing in Miss Minnie's path, "what would you like us to do with this casserole?"

"Well, obviously," Minnie said, "I'm going to take it inside and heat it up and dish it out." She looked back at Long John, and for the first time, hesitancy came into her voice and manner. "If you'd like, John," she said, "I could stay and eat with you."

Long John glanced down at Beatrice, reached for her hand and squeezed it. Then he came over to where Minnie and Carson were engaged in a standoff, him blocking the way to the house and her trying to get past him, and both of them trying to smile.

"Minnie," Beatrice called, her voice gentle, "it's getting colder. I think we should head on home."

"But—"

Long John took the casserole dish. "Thank you kindly," he said. "I'll enjoy this tonight and for the rest of the week. For now, though, I'm going to take a nap."

Minnie turned to Carson as if to get his support.

"I'm sure you understand Long John's need to rest," he said gently. "It was kind of you to bring him food. The true spirit of Christmas."

She narrowed her eyes and tilted her head as if trying to gauge his sincerity. Then she turned her palms up, spun and marched back to the SUV.

Carson and Long John waved to Beatrice and then watched the two women drive away.

"Close call," Long John said. Then he winked at Carson. "Sometimes it's the quiet ones who have something to offer. You remember that."

Carson lifted an eyebrow. "Something going on with you and Beatrice?"

"I wish," Long John said. "Maybe I was referring to our new friend Lily. Penny tells me your first wife was the dramatic sort. That Lily, though, she has a lot going on underneath."

Carson didn't answer. What could he say?

"You're not the only one who has things to deal with in the past," Long John persisted. "At least according to what Penny told me, Lily has had it rough."

That made Carson wince. He'd been so preoccupied with Lily's secrets about Pam that he'd neglected to offer her the pastoral counseling Penny had requested he do.

As he headed inside to collect the girls, he resolved that he'd make progress toward that before the day was out.

Chapter Six

As the sun set on Christmas Day, Lily walked toward her cabin, tired but feeling better.

Photographing the dogs for her school project had been fun. She'd posed one of the dogs near an old tractor in the barn, and another on a plaid blanket she'd found. Two big dogs, a black Lab and an Irish setter mix, had gotten in a play fight when she'd let them out into the fenced area. She'd taken photo after photo, knowing they'd look amazing against the snow with the mountains in the background.

Keeping busy with the dogs had helped to distract her from the news that Pam was pregnant when she'd died. That was what her therapist said to do when the past threatened to overwhelm her. Distract, and think about something else, something positive.

She'd memorized a Bible verse from Philippians about that, during her darkest days, and now she recited it in a whisper. "Whatsoever things are true, whatsoever things are honest, whatsoever things are just, whatsoever things are pure, whatsoever things are lovely, whatsoever things are of good report; if there be any virtue, and if there be any praise, think on these things."

Right now, the lovely things in her mind consisted of the hot bath she planned to take. The novel she'd read until she dozed off.

A lot of people were facing cranky kids and a big mess right about this time on Christmas. Lily, on the other hand, had pleasant time to herself. She'd revel in it and push away the sad information about Pam and the tug she'd felt toward family life, courtesy of Carson and the twins.

As she passed Long John's cabin, the front door burst open and Carson emerged. He was carrying a sleepy-looking Skye and had Sunny by the hand.

"You sure you want to take them along?" Long John was asking from the doorway.

"I think it's best." Carson's voice was tense, and when she looked more closely at his face, she saw deep vertical creases between his brows.

He glanced over at Lily, gave a quick, distracted wave, and then his phone buzzed. He held it to his ear and talked in short bursts, his forehead wrinkling tighter.

Something was wrong. As Carson hurried the girls toward their cabin, Lily stayed behind, looking up at Long John. "What happened?"

Long John leaned on his porch railing. "Someone from the church tried to take her own life today. She's in the hospital, and the rest of her family is having trouble coping."

"Oh, how awful!" Lily's chest ached for them. "On Christmas. Wow."

Long John nodded. "The family called Carson, and of course, he's going down to pray with them."

"I wonder if there's any way I could help. Maybe I can watch the girls for him."

Long John shook his head. "I offered, but he says he's going to take them down. They'll visit with their friend—this woman, she has a little boy, Gavin, who's six—while Carson talks to the husband and grand-parents."

Lily sucked in a breath. Exposing the twins to a situation that was hard for adults to understand just didn't seem right. She waved to Long John and then hurried after Carson, reaching him as he was ushering the girls into the car. "Hey, hold up a minute."

"Emergency with one of our church families." He closed the truck's back door as the girls strapped themselves in. "I have to get to town."

"It's about that." She stepped in front of him as he headed for the driver's seat. "Long John told me what happened. If being at the hospital will upset the girls, I'd be glad to watch them up here."

He forked fingers through his hair. "I'd love that, except that the girls overheard some details, and they're insisting on going. It's their friend's mom, you see. And they...well, because of Pam, they tend to get sort of anxious in any kind of family emergency, and they don't like to be away from me. I just..." He threw up his hands, looking frazzled. "I just think it's better I take them."

"Then let me come," Lily said impulsively. "I can watch out for them, feed them, whatever you need." She owed Pam's family any help she could offer.

His eyebrows lifted. "You'd do that for me?"

"Of course."

A little bit of the tension eased from his shoulders. "That would be great."

So they headed to town, Carson driving smoothly and safely, but fast. He allowed the girls to watch a movie in the back of the vehicle, apparently a rare treat, and they both wore headphones and were soon rapt.

"So, can you tell me what happened?" she asked after ascertaining that the girls were engrossed and not listening.

He shook his head. "This is a family that's been having some hard times," he said. "She lost her job, and she's been separated from her husband for a while. Money was tight this Christmas and…well, for some people, the holidays aren't happy." He sighed. "Honestly, I don't understand it myself. But I'll provide what comfort I can."

"That must be hard," she said while her mind raced. "Is she all right?"

"She's going to be. But it's hard for her family," Carson said. "I've only been in this situation a few times before, but I know people tend to blame themselves."

"They do." She felt like Carson was talking to her directly.

He swerved to avoid a branch lying on the road and then turned the car away from Esperanza Springs. "This is a regional hospital that serves several communities here. I'm not too familiar with it, but hopefully, they'll have a playroom or something for the kids to do."

Once out of the car, the twins clung to Carson, and Lily saw what he'd meant about unusual situations scaring them. Gone were the confident little girls who'd run all over the ranch. In their place were scared, nervous, teary kids.

Carson located the family in the waiting room and then turned to the twins. "I'm going to need to talk with the grown-ups for a little while," he said. "You can say hello, and then Miss Lily will help you and Gavin find somewhere to play quietly."

The little girls nodded, eyes wide.

Inside the small, dim waiting room, a gray-haired couple who must be the poor woman's parents, and a distraught-looking man—her estranged husband, maybe?—stood talking while a little boy hunched over a phone game in the corner.

Lily watched as Carson waded in. With his quiet questions and a hug for the older couple, he changed the atmosphere in the room.

Lily's heart squeezed, watching him. He'd confided to her that he didn't know what to do, and yet he was acting sure of himself, just what people needed in a pastor.

But while the adults' tension noticeably decreased with Carson's words, the children's didn't. The little boy abandoned the phone he'd been playing with and ran to bury his head in the man's leg, confirming Lily's impression that this was the boy's father. Sunny and Skye clung to Carson's hands.

Time to take action. She stopped a passing aide. "Is there a play area for children who are visiting?"

He shook his head. "The only thing we've got is an area for the siblings of patients in our children's ward."

"Could the kids play there for a little while?"

"You'll have to ask the nurses in that area."

Lily thought about it. Lots of the hospitalized kids

were most likely home for Christmas, along with their siblings. And this situation was unusual, an emergency. A little boy desperately needed a distraction.

She went back into the waiting room and sat on the edge of a chair, gesturing to the twins. "Skye, Sunny," she said. "Would you like to go exploring? We can stop and get some hot chocolate in the cafeteria." She didn't want to promise them a play area if one wasn't forthcoming.

"Okay." Both girls nodded, but they also seemed reluctant to let go of Carson.

She beckoned them in, as if to listen to a secret. "Go talk to Gavin and ask him to come," she said, "while I speak to his daddy."

They nodded and hurried over to the little boy while Lily introduced herself to Gavin's father. She explained what she was doing and where they'd be, so intent on helping that she forgot that she was a stranger in this community and inexperienced with kids.

The distraught father looked down at his son, who was now asking if he could go along. He lifted his hands, palms up. "Okay, um, sure, if Sunny and Skye are going."

As she turned to shepherd the children out of the room, she felt a hand on her shoulder. Carson. Heat rose in her face as she turned. "Thank you," he said, his eyes crinkling as they looked directly into hers. "That's just what they need."

Okay. She officially had a crush on this man. "You have my cell number, right?"

"Give it to me," he said, and she typed it into his phone.

He squeezed her hand briefly as he took the phone back, and Lily's heart rate accelerated.

They found the playroom, and when Lily explained the situation to a passing nurse, she readily opened it. Soon the children were oohing and aahing over the new-to-them toys, and Lily had a chance to think.

She really, really liked Carson. She had to acknowledge it now. But that just made things more complicated.

Because what if the unexpected happened, and he wanted a relationship with her? What if they got involved?

She'd have to tell him the truth about Pam and what had happened. Even she, who wasn't especially experienced with or good at relationships, knew that having a secret like that at the center would destroy anything they attempted to build.

But telling him would hurt him terribly. Even worse than she'd initially thought, given that Pam had been pregnant.

Lily watched the twins help their friend put together a racetrack for some little plastic cars.

Pam should have tried harder.

As soon as she had the judgmental thought, she pushed it away. Pam must have been going through so much pain. And yes, she'd masked it with lots of partying—partying that, Lily realized now, had put her unborn child in jeopardy—but pain was pain, and Lily knew from her father that drinking was more of a symptom than a base problem. It was a way to self-medicate.

Poor, poor Pam.

If only Lily had paid more attention, tried to find ways to help her.

Pushing away her own dark thoughts, Lily focused on the children playing at her feet and realized that little Gavin was running over a small plastic figure with his race car, over and over.

"Gavin, stop!" Skye put out a hand to protect the battered figurine.

"No!" Gavin pushed her hand away and ran over the doll again.

"You're hurting her!" Skye started to cry.

That got Sunny's attention away from her own race car. "Gavin, quit it!"

Lily sank to the floor in the midst of the children. "Hey. Let's play nice with the cars."

"This lady doesn't want to be alive," Gavin insisted, running his car into the doll again.

Out of my depth here. Why had Lily thought she'd be able to help this poor child? "Hey, Gavin," she said, "let's go see what we can cook on the stove. What's your favorite food?" She waved an arm to the plastic kitchen set.

"Don't wanna cook," Gavin said, turning his back to all of them.

Skye and Sunny looked more distressed.

"Girls," Lily said, "I'm going to give you a job. Please cook a pretend meal for all four of us and set the table. Gavin and I are going to talk a little, and then we'll come eat whatever you've fixed for Christmas dinner."

"Okay," Sunny said doubtfully. "Come on, Skye."

"He was hurting my doll," Skye said, hands on hips.

Lily gave her a stern look and pointed at the stove. To her amazement, it worked.

The girls occupied, she turned back to Gavin, who

was still banging his car into the doll. She was no psychologist, but she'd had some bad Christmases and some childhood struggles. "Christmas wasn't much fun this year, huh?" she said, picking up a car and running it aimlessly along the track.

"No!" He banged the doll hard with his car.

"I guess that makes you mad," she said.

"Mommy didn't get me any presents," he said, his lower lip out. And then suddenly, big tears welled up in his eyes. "I yelled at her and she almost died!"

Her heart constricted as she realized that he was blaming himself. Should she hug him, pull him into her arms? But she barely knew him. She reached out and patted his arm instead. "Sometimes grown-ups do things that are hard to understand," she said, "but what happened to your mom isn't your fault."

"I yelled at her a *lot*," he confessed, more tears rolling down his cheeks. "And then she went into her room and shut the door and then the amb'lance came and took her to the hospital."

Hard to argue with a six-year-old's concept of cause and effect, but she had to. "I yelled at my mother sometimes," she said. It was no exaggeration; she'd been awful as a teenager. "I feel really sorry about it, but parents understand. Kids are allowed to get mad."

There was a rustle beside her, and Skye came and knelt beside Gavin, patting his back. "I yelled at my daddy two days ago," she said. "And Sunny yells at him *all the time*."

"Did he die from it?" Gavin asked, gulping through tears.

"No. He's strong."

"Kids yelling never makes adults die," Lily said

firmly. "And your mommy is going to be okay. There are good doctors here who will help her feel better."

"Aunt Biddy said I might have to go away," he whispered, looking anxiously at Lily.

Lily felt like throttling Aunt Biddy. "Do you ever stay with your daddy?" she asked.

He nodded. "Wednesdays and Saturdays," he said.

"Hmm. Do you ever stay longer with him, like if your mom is sick?"

He nodded. "When Mommy was going to have a baby, I stayed with him a lot. But then she didn't have a baby after all."

Oh.

A miscarriage. Hormonal fluctuations. Christmas. Her heart went out to the poor woman who'd been in enough pain to overdose on pills.

"Maybe you'd stay with your daddy again for a while," she said, thinking of the man who'd agreed for her to bring Gavin down here. He'd seemed kind and concerned. But she didn't want to promise Gavin anything. You didn't make promises to kids unless you could keep them.

"When our mommy was gone at Christmas," Skye volunteered, "we made her cards."

Bless the child. "Let's go eat our pretend Christmas dinner," Lily said, "and then we'll make cards for your mom. I bet that will cheer her up a lot."

"Okay," Gavin agreed, and went gamely over to the table to partake of the plastic food Sunny had arranged.

A short time later, she heard the sound of a throat clearing at the half door, and Lily looked over and saw Carson. Since the children were occupied at the little table, she went over to stand by him. "How are things going?"

He ran a hand through his hair, mussing it. "Not great. She's stable, but the rest of the family is struggling to understand what happened." He nodded toward the children. "Looks like you did a better job with them than I did with the adults."

"I'm sure that's not true."

"I have a hard time with this particular issue," he said. "Especially talking to the survivors. Even the attempt is such a slap in the face to them."

Lily's stomach turned over. "Sometimes," she said, because she felt like she needed to say something, "people think their families will be better off without them."

Carson gestured at the children. "How could any mother think her child would be better off without her? How could Hannah—" He gestured toward the other wing of the hospital. "How could she plan to leave her son alone in the world?"

Lily let her head drop and stared at the floor. "I don't know, Carson," she said. "I just don't know."

He hadn't done enough, Carson berated himself as he exited the hospital behind Lily and the girls.

The three of them swung their linked hands, and Carson was torn between enjoying the fun they were having, worrying about the girls' attachment to Lily and wishing he were better at helping people dealing with such an incomprehensible situation.

A group of carolers approached the nursing home next door, and Carson recognized several of them from his church. So did the girls. "Can we go see Renee and Jackson?" Sunny asked, poised to run.

"If you walk on the sidewalk," he said.

The girls took off, walking rapidly, and he watched until he could see that Jackson's mother had greeted the girls and waved at him.

Lily stood beside him. "You okay?" she asked.

He shrugged. "Wish I'd done a better job in there," he said. "I had a hard time finding the right words, either for Hannah or her family. Like I said, it just doesn't make sense to me. How could a young mother with everything to live for try to take her own life?"

Lily's throat worked as she looked at him, distress obvious on her face. He wasn't impressing her, but he couldn't seem to stop himself from confiding. She was such a good listener.

"The truth is, ministers are just people," he continued on, because it helped to talk about it all. "Good at some things and not at others. Some are great preachers but can't do counseling. Some do beautiful funerals. Some are great with the sick, others with kids."

"You seem like you're good at most things."

That she thought so made him happier than it should, so he pulled himself back to earth. "Not what went down in there."

"How'd you leave the situation with them?" she asked.

He reflected. "Actually, her husband, who's been estranged, seems to want to help her, maybe even try to save their marriage. I think the potential loss of her hit him hard. As well, the impact it would have on his son."

"That's good," she said. "And I'll bet you set up counseling for the woman, right?"

He nodded. "Not just now, but into the future awhile."

"Then those are some good outcomes," she said. "Maybe their marriage will pull through." She thought a minute, then added, "My parents had a whole lot of ups and downs, but they stayed together until the end. Marriage isn't easy."

"True," he said. He paused, then added, "Pam and I… I don't know if she told you, but we had our share of problems."

She opened her mouth and shut it again.

He was about to say more when the carolers started yelling for his attention.

"Hey, Pastor C!" Jessie Malton called. "Why don't you join us?"

"Yeah, come sing!" another added.

Carson glanced over at her, then lifted his hands, palms up. Truthfully, he'd welcome the chance to be in a situation where he felt more comfortable and competent. He walked over toward the carolers, Lily trailing beside him. "What are you guys doing? Where are you headed?"

"Singing at the nursing home," Vance Richards said. "We could use your baritone."

"Can we go, Daddy?" Skye tugged at one of his hands, making puppy-dog eyes up at him.

"Please?" Sunny did the same.

He glanced over at Lily. "Do you mind staying in town a little longer? It might be fun for the girls."

And help them forget the sadness of the hospital.

She nodded, smiling her understanding. "It's fine, just as long as I'm not expected to carry a tune."

They followed the group inside, and as everyone

got organized and lined up the kids, he found himself off to one side with Lily. He touched her arm. "Look," he said, "I'm sorry I've been talking so much about Pam. I didn't mean to push you to tell me every detail of your friendship. I feel like I haven't been much of a pastor to you."

She waved a hand. "You have no obligation to me."

Conveniently ignoring his comment about Pam, but he wasn't going to focus on that anymore tonight. He did wonder, though, why she was so dismissive of her own needs and concerns. If he got the chance, he'd follow up with her.

For now, they followed the carolers into the rec room, where a large Christmas tree stood in the corner. Residents, some in wheelchairs, others helping to decorate the tree, looked up and waved. One man who was slumped in a chair, apparently asleep, lifted his head at the excited voices of the children.

The staff wore Santa hats and reindeer antlers, and several of the residents sported Christmas sweaters. Above the sound of a woman's rattling coughs, Carson heard violin music and looked toward the corner of the room where a frail, elderly man played with beauty and grace.

There were the usual nursing home smells, and he watched his girls to see that they were doing okay, weren't going to blurt out something rude. But they seemed a bit in awe of the new environment, and the scent of pine branches predominated as they moved farther into the room, near the large live Christmas tree.

They sang several carols, and the elders and some of the staff joined in. Carson glanced over at Lily and was pleased to guess from her gentle smile that she was enjoying the moment as much as he was.

Even in the face of all the pain they'd seen at the hospital, there was Christmas joy to share.

After half an hour, the carolers broke up into smaller groups and visited residents who couldn't leave their rooms. Lily and Carson ended up together—okay, because he angled for it—visiting several patients too ill for the children's noise and energy. They took turns reading the Bible and praying with individual residents, and it occurred to Carson: Lily was someone he'd like to minister with. She was so calm, so attuned to the needs of others.

As they strolled out into the hall, now quiet and deserted, he put a hand on Lily's arm. When she turned, her face was bright, her eyes aware. And he'd never seen anyone more beautiful.

He felt such warmth, for his girls and for Lily, too. He didn't know what to do with all his feelings.

"I know you were Pam's friend," he said, "but I'm starting to see you as more. That was…" He gestured back toward the rooms they'd visited. "That was good to do with you."

Her cheeks went pink and she nodded. "I liked it, too."

He glanced up and down the deserted hall and then turned toward her, taking her face into his hands. "A Christmas kiss?" he asked.

She didn't refuse. Her eyes shone like jewels as she looked up at him.

He drew her close and kissed her.

Chapter Seven

The nursing home sounds, the realization that it was Christmas, thoughts of the twins…everything faded away as Carson kissed her. Lily's heart pounded as the feelings swept and swirled inside her.

After an hours-long moment, he held her shoulders, lifted his lips from hers and touched her face with one finger, his warm, kind eyes just inches away from hers. "Ah, Lily," he said. "Lily, what have you done to me?"

Her lips curved into a smile as she savored the tenderness between them. No thoughts, just warm feelings. So this was what people wrote songs about; this was what made the music swell in romantic movies. "I don't take credit. It's you doing this to me."

At the end of the hall, the *clink* of a cart and a staff member's cheery greeting at the door of a resident's room alerted them that they weren't alone anymore. Carson took a step back. "I hope that was okay," he said, his eyes still intent on hers. "It was more than okay with me."

Lily's breath felt shallow, and her heart pounded out a jazzy rhythm. How was she supposed to answer his question? And yet the kiss had been wonderful, and she wanted him to know it. She let herself nod, let herself smile.

His eyes flickered down to her lips, and she drew in a breath. This was happening fast.

Too fast. She drew in another breath as reality pushed back in.

This was Pam's husband. Lily didn't deserve to enjoy his kiss.

Confusion washed over her. She didn't want to even think about what it all meant, but she knew she'd have to. "We should find the others," she murmured.

"We should." He draped an arm around her shoulders as they turned toward the lobby, and again Lily's breath caught.

Being close to Carson felt like the fulfillment of every romantic dream she'd ever had. She let herself lean into him, relishing the heartfelt emotions swimming through her.

And yet. And yet.

She couldn't let herself forget that this was Pam's husband. Pam was dead, but she, Lily, had to keep Pam's secret so as not to hurt Carson and the twins.

"Are you okay?" he persisted, his breath warm on her ear.

"I…I *guess* so, but… I have to think about all of it." She glanced up at him. "I'm not sure it's a smart thing, letting in those feelings."

His face seemed to fall. He straightened, putting distance between them. "That's wise. I should think, too. I'm supposed to be counseling you, not kissing you."

She stared. "Counseling me? Why?"

"Because Penny wanted me to…" He broke off.

She stopped and turned to face him. "Penny wanted you to what?"

"Oh, nothing. It's nothing. Just…get to know you. Befriend you, and see if there was anything I could do to help you."

She put a hand on her hip. "Did that include kissing me?" But almost immediately, her indignation turned into embarrassment. It was like that time when the teacher in her new fifth-grade class had assigned two girls to "make Lily feel at home." Forced friendships hadn't worked then, and they didn't work now.

"Hey." They were almost to the lobby now, the sound of voices and music penetrating the private space they'd been in. "What rabbit hole are you going down?"

She shook her head. "Nothing. It's fine."

"It's what I said, isn't it?" He smacked his own forehead. "What a smooth operator I am, huh? I kiss this beautiful woman, and it doesn't take but five minutes before she's wishing she'd never met me."

He was being funny, self-deprecating, but it almost sounded like he believed his own story. That couldn't be, though, could it? Surely Carson had confidence in himself, as attractive and charming as he was.

"I didn't kiss you because of what Penny asked me to do," he said. "That was my very own idea. Maybe not a wise one, in retrospect, but I can't say I regret it."

They were about to walk into the lobby, and she turned to him, putting a hand on his arm to stop his forward movement. "Look, Carson…that was lovely, but…you're right, it probably wasn't wise. We should go home as soon as we can, and maybe keep a little distance."

So I don't blurt out the truth to you.

His lips pressed together, and his posture stiffened. "You're still doing the rest of our photography session tomorrow?"

Oh, no. She'd forgotten about that obligation. "Right," she said. "It shouldn't take long, and then…"

"And then you'll pull away again?" He leaned closer. "Lily, I'm sorry if I wasn't as smooth as I should have been, and I'm really sorry if I've in some way offended you or hurt your feelings. That's the last thing I want. But—"

"Daddy!"

"Miss Lily!"

The twins came running and flung themselves on Lily and Carson, practically quivering with excitement.

"Come see our craft we made!" Sunny begged, tugging at Lily. "I made one for Daddy, and Skye made one for you."

Lily's heart seemed to swell inside her chest as she let Sunny tug her over to a low table. On it, reindeer made of Popsicle sticks and glitter sat drying.

Conflicting emotions flooded Lily's consciousness.

She wanted this. Wanted the excited kids and the messy crafts and the handsome man who cared for her.

But she didn't deserve it. All of this was Pam's, not hers. And if Pam couldn't have it, then no way should Lily. She needed to back off. For her own sake, for Carson and for the girls.

It would be a whole lot easier if she didn't have a photo shoot with them tomorrow.

* * *

The next morning, after she'd procrastinated by cleaning her already immaculate cabin and checking her email and social media multiple times, Lily gathered her photography equipment and headed over to Carson's cabin.

Her nerve almost faltered on the way there.

She'd spent the night tossing and turning, thinking alternately about how wonderful it had been to kiss Carson and how weak and vulnerable she'd felt afterward. Especially when she'd learned that Penny had asked him to check on her and counsel her.

Carson was the kind type and would do his duty by anyone in need. No, he wouldn't consciously decide to romance the lonely female veteran next door, but on some level, maybe that was what he had had in mind.

How humiliating. Best to get this photo shoot done and over and hurry on out of there. Protect herself. Stay in her cabin and with the dogs and refocus on why she was here.

And the reason for that had changed. She knew, now, that Pam had been wrong about Carson, that he was a wonderful father for his girls.

Which made Lily's unhappy knowledge about Pam's last days even worse. Hurting someone like Carson seemed unforgivable. She couldn't let it happen. She couldn't let the little family get any more embedded in her heart.

She had just one more obligation: a photo shoot with them as a way of paying her rent.

She needed to make more progress on her senior project. She was here to photograph dogs, not kiss a man.

That was what men and romance could do to a woman—take her off course. Make her dependent and weak, as her mother had been.

Carson opened the door, dressed in a flannel shirt and jeans, and the circles under his eyes suggested he hadn't slept any better than she had.

But they didn't detract from his rugged good looks. Her mouth felt too dry to speak.

"Let me help you," he said, immediately reaching for her things. "I would have carried that stuff over here."

She shrugged but handed him her lighting screen and lens bag. Then she followed him inside, where a delicious bacon smell and two pajama-clad little girls drew her like a magnet.

The twins jumped up and hugged her, their warm, sticky hands clutching, their faces bright. Then they both let go and settled back down to their bacon and pancakes.

She'd interrupted their breakfast, which made her feel awkward and out of place. "I'm sorry," she said to Carson. "I can see you've been sleeping in. I should have texted first. We can wait until later. I thought, with little ones…"

"That we'd be up early? Usually, yes, but yesterday was pretty busy and a late night. Want some breakfast?"

"No, it's okay," she said, watching Sunny pour an excessive amount of syrup over her flapjacks, turning the butter into a cloudy pool.

"Are you sure?" He lifted an eyebrow, his lips quirking into a smile. "I'm not exactly a master chef, but I do good pancakes."

"They're *super*good," Sunny said through a big mouthful.

"Sunny. Manners." Carson's correction was gentle, tinged with laughter.

And that was the problem with Carson and his girls—they were impossibly tempting. "All right, you talked me into it. I'll have a plate. Everything looks and smells so good."

"Right here." Skye patted the chair beside her.

And just like that, she was a part of the family again.

The problem being, that was exactly what she shouldn't be. And a sleepy, stubbly Carson who'd kissed her like he meant it last night was hard for her to resist.

Not to mention his adorable girls, whom she was coming to care for more with every hour she spent with them.

Not good.

Carson handed her a plate and then leaned back against the counter, forking a hand through his hair in what she was starting to realize was a habitual gesture. Possibly a sign he was stressed.

"Aren't you eating?" she asked him.

He shook his head. "I will later. I like to get the girls fed and settled first."

And get chores like me out of your way. "I was thinking—oh, wow, this is so good—anyway, I was thinking we could do a few shots in front of the fire, and some others by the Christmas tree. It shouldn't take long."

"Should we wear our Christmas dresses?" Skye asked.

"Hmm." Little girls in fancy dresses were always adorable. "What do you think, Dad? Do you want casual family photos or dressed-up ones?"

Instead of answering, Carson went over to the Christmas tree and pulled off an ornament. He showed it to her. "That's the last family photo we had made," he said. "It's a little, I don't know, stiff?"

Lily studied it while her heart pounded. Carson, Pam and the twins as babies. Their pose was definitely artificial, with Pam leaning forward behind a seated Carson while the twins sat, each on a knee.

But Pam was smiling with what looked like real happiness. So was Carson.

The photo nagged, pounding in her own role in Pam's death, a role she was too cowardly to describe to Carson—especially when it would mean causing pain to him and the girls. "You want something more laid-back?" Her voice sounded breathless.

"I think so," Carson said as he began carrying empty plates to the sink. "We're really not a dress-up kind of family. Even at church, most weeks, the girls go casual. I do, myself, when I can get away with it."

The twins were conferring. "We want to wear our dresses," Sunny announced. "Please, Daddy?"

"How about a compromise?" Lily pushed back one of Sunny's stray curls, and when the little girl let her face linger in Lily's hand, leaning against her, Lily gave her a little hug before letting go.

These girls needed mothering, badly.

Or maybe it was Lily who needed to mother. "Let's do casual pajama pictures by the Christmas tree, and then some fancy ones by the fire."

"But Daddy's not wearing his pajamas," Skye objected.

Lily glanced at Carson, who was busying himself at the sink, and saw color rise up his neck. "I think daddies can just wear jeans and a shirt," she said quickly. The last thing she needed was for Carson to change into pajamas.

That, she definitely couldn't handle.

"And he could put his bathrobe on over them. That's what he does when it's cold, anyway."

"Perfect." Lily helped wipe the twins' faces and brushed their hair while Carson fetched a robe and straightened up around the small tree. Lily set up several shots and asked them to talk to each other naturally, which they mostly did, although Sunny kept mugging for the camera with a big fake smile.

Finally, Lily got one shot with both girls looking up adoringly at Carson and knew it was perfect.

"Okay, next the fancy ones." She wanted to get this over with as soon as possible, because watching Carson and the girls through the camera lens, seeing the kind of family she'd always dreamed of—and the family Pam should still be a part of—simply hurt too much.

"Will you come help us change?" Skye asked, leaning against her.

"Yeah, will you?" Sunny ran over and started tugging at Lily's hand, nearly knocking her camera to the floor.

Carson frowned. "I'll help. Leave Miss Lily be." Setting boundaries, obviously. He was the daddy. She was just the visiting photographer.

The twins seemed to recognize that he wasn't kidding, because they moved away from Lily and followed him up to the sleeping loft without a backward glance.

And that was as it should be. They were the family, and she wasn't. The sounds of the girls giggling and Carson's deep baritone in response, scolding and laughing, were not for her.

She breathed deeply and focused on the artistry of light and filters and angles, and by the time they came down, she'd arranged rugs and logs and a wooden chair in front of the fire, making a cozy background.

It took only a few minutes to get all of them smiling and being their attractive selves, especially when Lily thought of silly questions to ask them or told them to think about their favorite Christmas memories and share them. All three visibly relaxed, and Lily felt accomplished, pleased that she was able to capture their good looks and love for one another.

"That's it," she said, "unless you can think of another angle or pose."

She was talking to Carson, but Sunny answered. "Now you should be in the picture," she said, coming over to stand beside Lily.

"No, honey." Lily patted Sunny's shoulder and then refocused on the meters on her camera to avoid looking at anyone. "I have to take the pictures, not be in them."

"Can't you set a timer like our teacher does?" Skye was beside her now, too. "We really want you to be in the picture!"

Lily looked over at Carson and saw the same concern in his eyes that she was feeling. The girls were getting too attached to her, if they were trying to include her in a family photo again today. And the trouble was, she felt the same way about them. Combine that with the fact that Lily herself was getting pretty attached to Carson, especially after kissing him, and they were creating a recipe for disaster.

"No," she said, without being able to think of an excuse. "I can't. I'd better not. Your pictures are best with just you and your daddy."

Big tears welled up in Skye's eyes. "Don't you like us?"

"Of course I do!" Lily knelt and embraced both girls. "You're great girls, and I like you a lot. It's just that today we're doing family pictures. And I'm your friend, but I'm not in your family."

Carson cleared his throat. "I'll take a picture of you three on my phone," he said. "There's no reason you girls can't have a Christmas-tree picture with your new friend Miss Lily, too." He looked at her, concern creasing his brow. "Unless she doesn't want that."

Oh, boy. They were walking on eggshells here. "I'd love to have another picture with the girls." And she would. She would treasure it, always remembering this Christmas on the ranch and the feeling of belonging she had gotten here, however briefly.

So she lifted her face and tucked a girl under each arm and they all smiled for the camera, and Carson took several pictures. And Lily tried not to pretend that they were her girls, and Carson was her husband, and they'd spend the future together as a family.

When he was done, the girls both hugged Lily tight, and her eyes got a little teary. "I'd better go," she said. Even as she started to gather her equipment, she felt her heart sink. Maybe this was the last time she would see Carson and the girls. They had had this excuse to be together, but it was over. Soon, they would leave the ranch and go back to their normal lives in Esperanza Springs. And Lily would go back to her normal life. She'd finish her degree, as planned, and then go live…somewhere. Wherever the road took her; wherever she could find a job.

Suddenly, that didn't feel exciting and adventurous, but lonely.

She shoved her arms into her coat and gathered her bags. Carson had gone back into the kitchen area, washing dishes. The girls were whispering up in the loft.

"I'm taking off, girls," she called up to them. "Have a fun rest of the day."

Carson wiped his hands on a dish towel and took a few steps toward her. "Thank you so much for coming over and doing this for us," he said. "I never have enough pictures of myself with the girls. It was a really thoughtful gift for Penny to think of, and kind of you to do."

"I'll get you proofs as soon as I've taken a look at them." She wanted to touch them up, and maybe, just maybe, she was hanging on to a shred of hope of seeing the little family again.

The girls came clattering down the ladder, practically tumbling over each other, smiles creasing their faces. "We have an idea," Sunny said.

"Uh-oh," Carson said, rolling his eyes, but smiling at the same time. "Sounds like trouble. What's your idea?"

Both girls turned to Lily, holding hands. They walked up to her, close, and looked up, their faces sweet and engaging. Then Sunny looked over at Skye. "Ready?"

Skye nodded.

Both girls took deep breaths and then turned to Lily and recited: "Will you be our new mommy?"

Chapter Eight

You had one job to do: counsel a troubled young woman. And instead, you kissed her.

And now your girls want her to be their mommy.

Later the same day, Carson walked away from Long John's cabin toward the barn where the dogs were housed. Long John had been happy to have the twins visit for a little while. And Carson had been glad for them to focus on someone other than Lily.

Even now, two hours after that awkward moment when the girls had asked Lily to be their mother, he was beating himself up.

Why had he let their relationship with Lily go so far?

He knew why, though: because in some ways, Lily was perfect for them. She was so sweet, kind, good with the girls. She was beautiful, innocently attracting Carson's interest without even a hint of provocative clothing or behavior.

Nonetheless, she was hiding things about Pam, and Pam's death.

And in the end, a woman like Lily would never go

for a man like him. She'd started to back away almost the moment after he'd kissed her.

Sure, being in the mountains was fun for now, an adventure to a woman raised in the flatlands, but that would go stale soon. He'd seen it happen with Pam.

And when she got tired of this place, of him, of the girls, she'd leave. Well, that was her right. But what he had to do was keep a distance, avoid building the connection any further.

The potential for hurt was so great. His girls didn't need another loss in their lives.

He didn't need it, either.

He had to cut this relationship with Lily off, fast. A little pinch now was better than a huge, painful break later.

A sharp *CHEW-EE, CHEW-EE* sounded from a fence post, a bright-eyed songbird seeming to call Carson away from his own thoughts and into the world of nature. Obedient, Carson looked out over the wide-flung fields to the Sangre de Cristos, white against the sky's intense blue.

He sent up a prayer of thanks for the beauty of this place and for being able to stay here over Christmas with his girls.

He needed to think more about his blessings and less about Lily.

Christmases had been simpler when he'd been married and the twins had been small. The girls hadn't had difficult expectations to fulfill, as they had this Christmas.

Man, he'd screwed up. They'd really, really wanted a dog.

If they'd had a mother, maybe she would have seen

that and helped him figure out how to manage it. As it was, he'd been busy and scrambling and not paying enough attention, obviously. Single parenting was an ongoing challenge.

But had it really been that much easier when Pam was here?

When he remembered the two of them together at Christmas, his first thought was of her discontent. She'd always wished for parties and shows and bright lights, things that he, a country pastor, hadn't been able to provide. Even before the twins had been born, he hadn't been able to take some fancy trip at Christmas as she'd wanted to. One, because he couldn't afford it, and two, because he had to preach on Christmas Eve.

And three, honestly, because he didn't want it. Didn't want to get on a plane to go somewhere else and party the season away. He'd preferred to stay at home.

Boring, Pam would say.

Man, had they been ill-suited.

And it had contributed to Pam's problems, her increasing unhappiness. Surely he, trained in pastoral counseling, should have been able to help his own wife. But he hadn't. Hadn't realized how serious the situation was getting. Hadn't known how to stop the flood of her angry emotions and moods.

Hadn't been able to stop her from running away from him and the girls, albeit in the guise of military obligations.

He reached the kennels at the same time a truck pulled in and parked. Jack DeMoise jumped out, then opened the rear door to extract his year-old son.

"Thanks for coming up on the day after Christmas," Carson said to the veterinarian.

Jack shrugged. "Nothing else to do. Glad you were here to open the place up for me. When the ranch volunteers let me know that old Bella was having trouble, I wasn't sure how I'd get into the barn to see her."

Carson opened the door and they walked inside to the sound of loud barking, greetings from a plethora of dogs who all could use more attention than they normally got.

"Mind holding Sammy?" Jack asked.

Carson reached out and took the one-year-old into his arms, cuddling him close. Sammy's back was stiff and arched, his tiny hands on his ears.

"Those dogs are loud," Carson agreed with the baby, pitching his voice low and pacing, bouncing him gently. "They'll quiet down soon."

And it was true; their woofed greetings were already dying down, and the child settled, too.

Wish I could have another child.

And where had *that* thought come from? Pam hadn't wanted more children—honestly, hadn't initially wanted the twins; they'd been a surprise—and since her death, he'd had his hands full taking care of the girls. Normally, he didn't have an ounce of attention to spare to the idea of maybe having another child; witness his obliviousness to his daughters' expectation of a puppy. Besides which, thinking of a third child evoked painful thoughts of the unborn child who had died with Pam.

Now having another child would involve remarrying, obviously a complicated proposition.

Focus.

He watched as Jack knelt before Bella's cage, studying her before going in. He looked back up at Carson.

"Man, those volunteers are great. They keep this place clean. Helps prevent disease."

Carson sniffed and nodded, appreciating that the place smelled like disinfectant rather than the many other odors a group of dogs could produce.

"And they're sharp," Jack added. "They noticed Bella's problem quickly."

"Which is what?"

Jack undid the lock on the cage and eased in, soothing the big black dog as he knelt before her. "Aside from neglect and being thirteen years old, with parasites and some mammary tumors…she seems like she has an ear infection." He nodded at her. "See how she's pawing at her face and ear?"

Carson nodded. "What can you do for a dog who's that old?"

Jack studied the dog, his face thoughtful. "Quite a lot, actually. An antibiotic should wipe out this infection, and then we'll take on the tumors if need be. They're probably benign. What she really needs, though, is some tender loving care for her golden years."

"Is she likely to get adopted?" Carson stooped to look at the dog. "Akita, isn't she?"

"Uh-huh. And there are people who have open hearts for these hard cases." He glanced up at Carson. "Thanks for holding Sammy. You look like a natural with him."

"I love babies. If things were different, I'd like to have another," Carson admitted. To preclude Jack's asking questions, he asked one of his own: "How about you? Any urges toward another child?"

Jack snorted. "I worry about this one too much. I

couldn't handle another." He ran his hands over the dog. "Don't know how you managed as a single dad with two."

"Wasn't easy, but at least they were older when we lost Pam. You had Sammy alone almost from the beginning." He thought back over what Jack had said. "What do you mean, you worry about him too much? Is something wrong?"

Jack sighed, his forehead creasing. "Seems to me he's too quiet. Doesn't react the way I'd like to see." He frowned. "The last nanny thought he might be on the spectrum, but I can't get a doctor to corroborate it this early."

"Wow. I'm sorry, man. That's a lot for you to handle alone."

"Alone's how I'm going to be." Jack shrugged and continued his examination of the dog. "Never mind about me. What's going on with you? Heard you and your girls aren't up here by yourselves."

Carson glared. "No, we're not. Long John's here, too. In fact, that's where the girls are now."

Jack chuckled. "Heard there was someone even prettier than Long John."

Carson blew out a sigh. "Word does travel fast in a small town."

"When General Patton and Mrs. Barnes are involved, it does." Jack grinned. "Word on the street is, you like Penny's niece."

Now, who had said that? "I do like her," he revealed, "but that doesn't mean I'm getting involved with her." Even as he said it, he realized he was fooling himself. What had that kiss meant, if not involvement?

"Why not?" Jack shoulder-bumped him as they

walked to the front of the barn. "Don't you ever want someone to share your life?"

"Do you?"

"I'm different," Jack said, "and we're talking about you."

"I'd like the companionship," Carson admitted, "and I'd like a mom for my girls. But..." He sighed. "I didn't exactly do a bang-up job at marriage before. And I'd hate to have the girls learn to care for someone, then lose them."

"You can't let one bad marriage ruin you for the institution," Jack argued.

Carson noticed that he didn't dispute the idea that Carson's marriage had been bad. Did everyone in town know it, then?

"Everyone's not like Pam," Jack went on, pretty much confirming the notion. "Take this Lily, for example. Sounds like she's a nice person. Why don't you ask her out? Give dating a whirl."

"It's not that easy!" Carson thumped the wall, too hard, to push a loose board back into place. "Especially with someone like Lily. She's first class, man. Gorgeous, big heart, talented..."

"What, you're holding out for a loser?"

What could he say to that? Carson waved a hand to indicate he was done with the conversation, but Jack's words echoed in his mind. As he watched the man administer a shot to Bella, he had to admit he was mixed up inside.

He couldn't claim that he felt nothing for Lily. In fact, he'd kissed her and loved it. It was the first time he'd been drawn to anyone since Pam.

It wasn't just the kissing, either. Lily was fun and

funny and kind, warm and natural with his girls, with passions for photography and dogs that made her interesting.

But Lily was keeping secrets. What's more, he'd pledged to counsel her, not romance her, and he was doing a shoddy job of that.

And all of that was aside from the fact that a man like Carson just wasn't appealing or exciting enough for a woman like Lily, not long-term.

The door to the barn burst open, and there was the woman in question—with a twin holding either hand. He got to his feet, shifting the baby to his other arm. "You girls were supposed to stay with Long John," he scolded, not looking at Lily.

"We saw her walking by, and we wanted to come, and Long John let us," Sunny said.

"I'm sorry," Lily said. "I was coming to figure out my next photo session with the dogs. I didn't know whether to say yes, but they pleaded so hard..."

Jack chuckled. "Just imagine when they're teenagers."

"Dr. Jack!" The twins ran to him, clearly delighted. The fun-loving veterinarian was a favorite with them. "What are you doing here? Did you find a puppy for us?"

"He's not here for that." Carson sighed, feeling overwhelmed.

"It's fine." Jack introduced himself to Lily—now, why had Carson forgotten to do that?—and then invited the twins to watch as he finished up Bella's care. "Puppies are nice," he told them as he manipulated the old dog's back legs, checking her joints, "but there are dogs who need homes more. Puppies will always find a home. It takes a special family to love a dog like Bella."

"*I* could love her," Skye said. "She's pretty."

That was a stretch, but more power to Jack if he could steer the girls toward a senior dog. If Carson ever did give in to their pleas for a canine companion, it would be for one who really needed a home.

And who was calm, and didn't chew up shoes, and was house-trained.

But he didn't want a dog, he reminded himself. And he didn't want his girls getting any more attached to Lily, either. Didn't want to get more attached to the woman, himself. Didn't want to watch the way she put an arm around each girl as all three of them knelt in front of Bella's cage, listening to Jack explaining that you needed to be careful even around nice dogs, that you shouldn't get between a dog and its food.

It seemed to him that Jack was leaning too close to Lily, smiling at her a little too much. Heat rose in Carson's neck. Was the vet hitting on her?

Carson started over, but just in time, he caught himself. He had no right to feel possessive about Lily.

Annoyed, he walked toward the front of the barn, the part that served as an office, hoping to get a grip on himself.

Instead, he saw a bulletin board. The left-hand half was covered with photos of dogs who needed homes, while the right-hand half displayed families who'd already adopted a senior dog. Lots of happy-looking people, some of whom were friends of his.

If Carson were any fun at all, he wouldn't have disappointed his girls at Christmastime. He'd already have gotten them a dog, if not several pets.

But Carson wasn't any fun. Just ask the girls' mother.

In the couple of minutes it took Carson to compose himself, Jack got Bella from the cage and walked her outside, Lily and the girls following along. The girls giggled and clucked at the dog, and she turned and slurped one twin's face, then the other—she was basically the same height that they were.

Lily looked on, laughing with delight. The way her face lit up...

She glanced over, saw him watching and flinched. "I have to go," she said quickly, and headed away from the barn.

Automatically, Carson walked her to the gate.

Behind them came the sound of Sunny's high, clear voice: "Daddy doesn't want us to talk about this," she was saying to Jack, "but me and Skye want Miss Lily to be our new mommy."

Lily glanced at him, distress written all over her face. It matched the distress in his own heart.

He couldn't let his girls get hurt again.

When they got to the gate, he opened it and held it for her, shifting Jack's baby to his other arm. "Listen, Lily," he began.

"I'm sorry," she said at the same time.

They both stopped. Looked at each other, and their gazes tangled.

Best to do this quick. "Lily," he said, "you're a great person, but it would be better if you'd stay away from me and the girls."

Chapter Nine

The next day, just after Lily had cleaned up from the healthy lunch she'd forced herself to eat, she looked through the window and saw Carson walking out the door of his cabin.

Instantly, she was flooded with embarrassment and hurt.

It would be better if you'd stay away.

She didn't normally dwell on the times she'd felt unwanted: tiptoeing around her parents' arguments, trying to make friends at a new school, being assigned as the only woman in a work unit overseas.

But somehow, being told to stay away by Carson—from him *and* those sweet little girls—hurt a hundred times more.

She couldn't give in to the despair that threatened her, though. She had to make every effort to keep it at bay.

She dried her hands and went over to the spot in front of the fire where Bella, the old Akita, lay on a soft blanket.

Step one, when you were feeling bad: help someone else.

She rubbed the dog's ears for a few seconds, earning a feeble tail wag, and then grabbed her laptop and settled in at the little kitchen table.

Starting her online course early would keep her plenty busy, keep her mind from going places that wouldn't do her any good.

She'd just opened the welcome video from the instructor when there was a knock on her cabin door.

Her emotions stampeded out of the place she'd corralled them, because it couldn't be anyone but Carson.

She stood and drew in a deep breath. She'd send him away.

As she crossed the cabin, there was another knock. "I'm coming!" She grabbed the door and flung it open, but didn't step back for him to enter. "What can I do for you, Carson?"

He winced. "Could I come in and talk for a minute?" His eyes were concerned, studying her.

"Are the girls all right?"

"Yes, of course! They're down in town, at a party for one of their friends."

"Then what do you need?"

He sighed. "It would be easier if I could come inside."

Don't you know you're killing me? She opened the door and stepped to one side, arms crossed.

He closed the door behind him, rubbing his hands together and stomping the snow from his boots. Then he looked at her, his dark eyes sorrowful. "I've hurt you when I was supposed to help you. I'm sorry."

"I'm fine."

"It's not your fault my girls tend to get attached too easily. Probably, it's my fault."

"Happens a lot, does it?" The moment she said it,

she wished she could take it back. But she'd thought her connection with his girls was at least a little special.

"No," he said slowly. "They do tend to enjoy being around women, and to cling to their teachers. But the way they've latched onto you…no, it's never happened before, quite like this. They've grown so fond of you that they want to make it permanent. In fact, they're quite annoyed with me that I don't see the light."

She waved a hand. "Kids."

He blew out a breath. "I'm botching this apology. I think you're a very appealing woman—you can probably tell—and if things were different, I'd—"

"Don't, Carson. There's no need. I'm not interested in a relationship." She looked away, not wanting to see the relief on his face. "Anyway," she said, "it's nice of you to check on me, but I'm fine. I have coping mechanisms." She gestured toward the open laptop computer, the fire, the dog.

His eyes skimmed from one to the next, and then to her face. "Give me ten minutes to talk with you and I promise I'll get out of your hair."

There seemed to be no other option, unless she wanted to be outright rude. She gestured toward the couch and sat in the armchair kitty-corner from it. "Something to drink?" politeness made her ask.

He waved the offer away. "What made you take in Bella?" he asked.

"I wanted to help." She slid to the floor and reached out to run a hand along the dog's bony back. Bella thumped her tail and licked Lily's hand, and Lily's heart twisted.

"She needs help, from the looks of things."

Okay, she could spend their ten minutes talking

about Bella. It was probably better that way. "According to Jack," she said, "Bella was tied to a tree for years. You can see how worn away the fur is around her neck. And she has tumors from never having been spayed. She needs to regain strength before she can have surgery to have them removed. I figured, at least for the couple more days I'm here, I can give her some extra attention and love."

He looked from her to the dog and back again. "You put me to shame," he said quietly. "Here I've resisted getting a dog, and you're not even in the area for but a few days, and yet you're reaching out to an animal that needs care. I admire you for that."

She felt her cheeks heat at the unaccustomed praise. "I get as much out of it as Bella does. Right, girl? You're good company." Bella was keeping her from over-the-top sadness about how she'd started to fall in love with the idea of family, represented by Carson and his girls, an idea she was pretty sure she'd never get to realize herself.

"So," he asked, his voice sounding falsely cheerful, "you were in touch with Jack about this? Is that how you came to take the dog in?"

She looked up at him, confused by the tension in his voice. "Yes. Is that against the rules?"

"No. No, of course not." He shook his head and then rested his cheek on his clasped fists, leaning forward, staring out the window. "Jack's a good guy."

Lily felt her eyebrows draw together as she tried to puzzle out what Carson was saying and what he really meant. If she hadn't known better, she'd have thought he was jealous of her having contact with Jack. But that didn't make sense on any level.

"Listen, Lily," he said, "I've been remiss. I'm a pastor, and Penny wanted me to talk to you about your, well, your issues with the war and maybe even other stuff in your past. She didn't want me to tell you she'd put me up to it, but I let that slip, so I might as well be open about it now."

This again. Nothing like making her feel even more screwed up than she was. "You don't need to do that. I'm fine. Really. The military has good counselors, and I've taken advantage of that when I've needed to."

"Why do you think Penny wanted me to talk to you, then?"

Lily shrugged, but she knew, and as long as she'd given Carson ten minutes, she might as well tell him just to pass the time. "Penny is my mom's sister. She knows my mom wasn't the strongest person in the world, and that my dad has…issues."

"What kind of issues?"

"He's an alcoholic. Nowadays, he's addicted to opiates, too." The simple words choked her a little, surprisingly, and she clamped her mouth shut.

"That must be hard to deal with," Carson said.

She nodded and drew in a breath. "Sometimes."

"Like at Christmas?" he probed. "Where are your parents now?"

Lily cleared her throat. "Well, Mom, she…she passed away last year. My dad's in the Kansas City area, I think. Last I heard."

"You're not in touch?"

She shook her head. "Not much." Then, to cover up how guilty she felt about that, she shot him a glare. "Are you judging me? Believe me, I've tried to help him at various times, even though he made my mom's life a nightmare, and even though all he wants from me is money for booze and drugs. He won't admit he has a problem, though, and until he does—"

Carson held up a hand. "Whoa. I didn't mean to accuse you of anything. I'm sorry you've had to deal with all of that, and the last thing I would do is judge you. You've built a fine life for yourself."

Lily looked briefly around the cabin. "Yeah, with a stray dog and nowhere to go on Christmas. Some life." The bitter sound of her own voice shocked her and she clapped a hand over her mouth. "I didn't mean that! I have a lot of good things going for me."

"You're a kind person who's trying to improve her lot in life by getting a degree, and you still have room in your heart to help others," he said quietly. "In my book, that's a fine life."

She shrugged. "We all do what we have to do." She wanted to add a compliment to him—that he'd lost his wife and was managing to do a lot of good in the world despite that tragedy—but she was afraid it would come out wrong.

And she didn't want to bring up the subject of Pam.

"You never fell into drinking or drugging yourself?" His voice sounded elaborately casual.

She raised both hands like stop signs. "I didn't say that. I made my share of mistakes." Remembering some of her escapades, during her teen years and even her early twenties, made her blush and shake her head. "I was a wild child. That's why Pam and I…" She trailed off. Why had she brought up Pam?

"Why you partied together?" Carson didn't sound disapproving.

Lily hesitated, then nodded. "I'm not proud of the

way we acted, Carson. I wasn't comfortable with it even back then. And now that I know better, I'm even more ashamed."

"There's no condemnation in Christ," he said lightly. "Did she talk about our marriage?"

Lily blew out a sigh. Carson was obviously obsessed with finding out exactly how Pam had felt about him at the time of her death. How was she supposed to handle this? "A little."

"Did she tell you we had problems?"

She'd *told* Lily that Carson was an abusive husband, but that was obviously a lie.

What had been Pam's agenda, with all the lying?

Bella, bless her, chose that moment to stand up, her limbs shaky, and limp toward the cabin door. "I have to help her." Lily hurried across the cabin to open the door, and then she guided Bella down the steps. "Take your time," she muttered to the dog. Maybe Carson would forget his question.

After a moment, Carson came out the door and stood on the porch. "I guess I had my ten minutes and more," he said.

"Yeah." Lily forced a little laugh. "I should get back to work on my online course."

"I understand." He trotted down the porch steps and then stopped beside her. "Listen, Lily, I was wrong, and rude, to tell you to stay away. While you're up here, you're welcome to spend time with me and the girls."

She shook her head quickly. "I don't want them to get attached to me. I'm only staying a couple of days longer."

"I'll talk to them," he said firmly. "It'll be a good lesson for them, and…and pleasant for all of us, if you'd care to spend time together. As friends," he added quickly.

"Right," she said. "Friends."

Later that afternoon, Carson accepted Long John's offer of a hammer and nails and headed outside to continue the work on the cabin's porch.

His girls stayed inside the cabin with Long John... and Lily.

Carson blew out a sigh. He'd had a serious conversation with the girls over lunch, reminded them that Lily was a friend, not a potential new mother. Explained that if they kept making her uncomfortable by talking about her joining their family, she wouldn't be able to hang around with them.

They'd hastily agreed not to bring it up, said they understood, but Carson had his doubts. Still, when they'd seen Lily walking Bella outside, he'd allowed them to go out and say hello. It turned out they'd begged her to bring the big dog to Long John's to meet Rockette when they went over to visit. They'd developed a fantasy that the two dogs could be best friends.

Oh, well. It was better than the fantasy that Lily could be their mom.

Better than his own fantasy that Lily could be some kind of romantic partner to him.

He ran his hands over the ramp, inspecting the spot that had broken. If he could just shore it up with a couple of two-by-fours, it wouldn't look perfect, but it would be safe. Safe, at least, for now.

He was measuring boards when his phone buzzed. He checked the lock screen and smiled.

Finn Gallagher was the ranch manager and was fast

becoming one of Carson's good friends; in fact, in November, Carson had performed the marriage ceremony for Finn and his new wife, Kayla. The two had gone through a lot, both separately and together, but now they were deliriously happy, and so was Kayla's son, Leo, who'd found a true father figure in Finn.

"How's the south?" he greeted Finn, and they talked for a little while about Kayla's friends whom they'd visited before Christmas, and Finn's big family of brothers, with whom they'd stayed for the holiday itself. Apparently, Leo was having the time of his life with his new cousins, and the family had even welcomed Shoney, their blind and deaf cocker spaniel, as an honored visitor.

"So how's the ranch?" Finn asked, and Carson was able to report that the dogs were fine, that he was fixing Long John's porch and that his girls were keeping the older man company.

"Is that other guest doing okay?"

"Lily? Yeah."

"Great." Finn didn't pursue the subject; obviously, he wasn't in the gossip circuit.

Which, perversely, made Carson want to confide. "She's an…interesting woman."

"Oh?"

"My girls have really taken to her."

"That's good," Finn said, "because from what I've heard, it sounds like Pam wasn't really there for them. Or for you."

Finn's words, so blunt and matter-of-fact, echoed oddly in Carson's ears.

He'd spent so much time beating himself up about being a bad husband that he hadn't really considered

Pam's adequacy as a wife and mother. And that was okay; it was good to be nonjudgmental, right?

But he had to admit that Finn was right. Pam had spent most of her time overseas, even after the girls were born. Especially after the girls were born, even when she'd had the option to take a job stateside.

She'd had many great qualities, but she hadn't been enthusiastic about motherhood.

Nor about being a wife.

And while he could blame himself for the latter, he could never blame his lovable girls for their mother's lack of interest. They'd done nothing to deserve her neglect.

A tiny voice inside him whispered that maybe, just maybe, he hadn't deserved that, either. Maybe her lack of interest in him and the girls had more to do with her issues than with Carson's inadequacies.

"You still there?" Finn asked. "Hey, I shouldn't have said that. Sorry."

"No, it's fine. You might have a point."

And Carson had some more thinking to do. They talked a little longer, and then Finn rang off, saying he'd see Carson in a few days.

And that reminded Carson that this interlude alone on the ranch, with Long John and Lily and the girls, would come to an end. They'd be back into their busy lifestyles. Lily would be gone.

The thought brought a big bank of mental black clouds, so he was grateful to hear Long John thumping out of the house, using his walker to get to the porch.

"Haven't made much progress, have you?" Long John asked, ragging him. "You getting paid by the hour or something?"

"If I could have some…" Carson broke off. He'd been about to make a joke about how it would be nice to have some help, but Long John just wasn't able.

The older man seemed to know what Carson was going to say. "Believe me, I'd help if I could. I hate being all crippled up."

"I know you would. You do a lot for me, including watching out for the girls. Are they okay?"

"Having a lot of fun with Lily and the dogs." Long John paused. "You know, you and I both have some problems in the past, but I think it's about time we tried to overcome 'em."

"Yeah?" Carson stayed focused on leveling a board and sliding it into place.

"Yeah. You need to get over that wife of yours. Face the truth about her. Deal with it."

Not again.

Long John was right, and Finn was right. Carson had things to work on. But he didn't necessarily want the older man's advice right now.

He focused on the other man. "I know what problems I have. What about you?"

Long John leaned a little closer. "Truth is, I'd like to ask someone out, but with my limitations…" He waved a hand at his walker.

"Is it Penny? I don't know that you should pursue her." Carson knew that both Long John and his friend Willie had a good-natured rivalry about the woman who owned the ranch. "She's still hung up on what happened with her husband. I don't think she's ready."

"I know that. That's not who I meant."

"Who, then?" He grinned. "Minnie Patton?"

Long John snorted. "She does make a fine tuna fish casserole, but no. Close, though."

Then Carson remembered. "Minnie's sister?" Long John had seemed to enjoy chatting with her.

Long John rubbed his grizzled chin and nodded. "Yep. She's a real sweet woman."

"I think you should do it. Ask her out. What can you lose?"

"I could ask you the same question," Long John said, neatly turning the tables. "You have some limitations yourself, but why let the past ruin the present for you?"

Carson *didn't* want to talk about Pam. "I'm not the most exciting man on the block," he said. And then he remembered Finn's off-the-cuff remarks about Pam. Maybe the lack of fun had been more about her restlessness than a personal trait of his.

"You need to deal with your past," Long John said. "Really face what happened with your wife and in your marriage."

Carson nodded. "You're probably right."

"That young woman in there might need just exactly what you have to offer," Long John said. "Maybe she's what your girls need, too. The good Lord works in mysterious ways."

"It's possible," Carson said. Then, figuring he had enough deep stuff to think about, he changed the subject.

They chatted easily about sports, the weather, fishing.

Until suddenly, there was growling, barking and a loud cry from inside the cabin.

Chapter Ten

At the sound of dogs snarling and girls screaming, Lily spun from Long John's refrigerator, where she'd been getting drinks for the twins. She ran toward the sitting area as the door opened from outside.

Rockette and Bella stood stiffly, several feet apart, Bella gulping down a treat, Rockette growling.

Behind them, both twins wailed.

"What happened?" Lily cried, running to Skye as Carson burst through the door and ran to Sunny.

"Bella bit me!" Sunny sobbed, clutching her hand to her chest. "Daddy, she bit me!"

Carson pulled Sunny into his lap. "Did you see what happened?" he asked Lily.

Lily shook her head, feeling two inches tall. "I'm so sorry. I was getting them something to drink." What had she been thinking, leaving two little ones alone with two big dogs? "I'm so sorry, I should have been watching them more closely. Skye, honey, are you okay?"

"I am, but Sunny's not," Skye sobbed.

"Let me see your hand," Carson said, his head bent over Sunny, cuddling her close.

Sunny held it out, and they all leaned forward to see…nothing. "Where does it hurt, honey?" Long John had come in behind Carson, and now he sat down on the edge of his recliner to better see the damage, or non-damage.

Sunny pointed to a spot on her hand, and when Lily leaned forward, she saw a tiny speck of pink. No broken skin. Relief bloomed in her chest.

In Lily's lap, Skye gulped away her tears and leaned forward to study her twin's hand. "I can't see anything."

"I think you're going to live," Carson said, the tension gone from his voice. "The skin isn't broken."

"I felt her teeth!" Sunny insisted. "Why did she bite me, Daddy? I thought she was nice!"

"Because you were teasing her with treats," Skye said. "Remember, Dr. Jack said to be careful with dogs and their food."

"I was just playing a game," Sunny said, an expression of annoyance replacing her tears. "I wanted to see which dog could get the treat first." She held her hand up in the air to demonstrate what she'd done.

"Big mistake, honey," Carson said. "Did you learn your lesson?"

"They're bad dogs!" Sunny frowned at Bella. "Especially you. Bad dog!"

"They're just doing what dogs do naturally," Long John said. "In the wild, back in the wolf days, they'd fight over every morsel in order to survive and feed their young."

"And Bella's been hungry a lot, from what Dr. Jack said," Carson added. "She's probably extra worried about getting enough to eat."

"I should never have brought Bella over," Lily said.

"I wasn't thinking about how she might compete with Rockette for food. They were getting along so well, but I shouldn't have left the girls alone with them, even for a minute." She didn't dare look at Carson. He must think she was the worst person ever, putting his precious girls at risk.

"It's my fault," Long John said. "I should have stayed in here to help you. These two are a handful!" He put a hand on each blond head.

"Look, I'm the one responsible for the girls. I'm sorry to leave you in charge like that," Carson said. "You couldn't have known what would happen."

Grace instead of blame. It was a new experience for Lily, and her heart melted.

"It's not Miss Lily's fault." Sunny scrambled out of Carson's lap and scooted over to lean on Lily. "She told us to be careful and gentle."

Lily sat, one girl on her lap and one beside her, her heart contracting painfully. She'd always claimed she didn't understand kids, was in no hurry to have her own, but these two had effortlessly won her heart.

She'd started to care for these girls as if they were her own. Any little hurt they had, she seemed to feel herself. She wanted to take care of them and comfort them and love them.

But they were Carson's girls, not hers. Carson's and Pam's. What right did she have to feel anything for them?

After Carson had left with the girls, Lily hesitated near Long John's door, her hand on Bella's collar. She hadn't wanted to go with Carson and the twins, impose herself on them, feel more attached. But she also didn't feel like being alone.

"I'd be obliged if you'd fix me a cup of tea," Long John called from his recliner.

"Sure!" Relieved, Lily hung her coat back up, went over to the kitchen area and turned on the kettle.

"Fix one for yourself, if you'd like," he said. "I'd welcome the company."

Something in his tone sounded artificial. Why was he encouraging her to stay? She marched over and faced him, propped a hand on her hip. "Are you just being nice?"

"Welllll…" He drew the word out, smiling a little. "I *would* like the company. But I think you've got something on your mind. If you want to talk about it, I'm available. Free and confidential," he added, a twinkle in his eye.

She couldn't help smiling back at the older man, and a couple of moments later she was sitting on his couch, two steaming mugs of tea on the table between them.

"So what's been on your mind, little lady?" He sipped his tea and gave an appreciative sigh.

On the floor, Rockette echoed it. Bella was nosing around the edges of the room.

The "little lady" label might have irritated her from some men, but not Long John. "Too much," she admitted. The situation with Carson and the twins had her head spinning with confusion, her heart raw and aching.

Tell him about Pam.

The idea seemed to come out of nowhere, but all of a sudden she wanted a sounding board. "You meant it when you said confidential?" she asked.

"Absolutely."

She took a sip of tea and then wrapped her hands around the cup. "I... Something happened when I was in the service."

He nodded and raised an eyebrow.

"I... This woman, another soldier..." Saying Pam's name, revealing her identity, seemed too scary. "A friend of mine, she and I had an argument. There was a lot that happened... Anyway, she was furious at me." She waved her hand, not wanting to go into the whole complex story. "But the end result was, she ran out of our guard hut and purposely got herself shot."

His bushy white eyebrows came together. "She make it?"

Lily shook her head. For just a moment, she relived the scene: Pam running off toward the oncoming vehicle. Lily's own shouts and those of their two fellow soldiers. They weren't supposed to leave the hut, but to stick together and inspect each vehicle entering their compound.

Lily remembered the *rat-tat-tat* of gunfire. Pam had stopped as if running into a glass wall. Her body had curled in on itself and then collapsed.

The other two had rushed after the fleeing vehicle. But Lily had gone to Pam. "When I got to her, she was already...gone," she said. And then her throat closed and her eyes burned and she couldn't say any more.

"And you blame yourself."

Lily nodded.

They sat for a moment, staring into the fire. And then Long John spoke. "When I was in 'Nam, I left a buddy in the jungle."

"How do you mean, left?"

"Turned tail and ran," he said. "Saved my own life."

From what she knew of the older man, she thought there was probably more to the story. "Was he down?"

Long John nodded. "Down, and in pretty bad shape. Felt like I had a choice—lose him or lose both of us." He spread his hands. "It dogged me for a couple of years, that I didn't choose right. Any grunt in the movies or on TV would've stuck around, even if just to bring his body home."

"Life's not like the movies or TV."

"No, it's not."

They sat in silence for a couple of minutes, but Lily was curious. Finally, she asked, "You said it bothered you for a couple of years. How'd you get over it?"

Long John stared into the fire. "Ever hear that expression 'confession is good for the soul'?"

"Uh-huh."

He turned his head and propped it on his folded hands, facing her. "I went to his twin brother, who also served. Told him the whole story."

"Wow." That had taken courage. "Was he angry?"

"Slugged me hard enough to break his own hand." Long John shrugged. "Can't blame him. Rick might've had a chance, if I'd been able to stay with him or drag him out of there. I was honest about that."

"Did his twin end up forgiving you?"

Slowly, Long John nodded. "He did more than that."

"What do you mean?"

Long John gestured toward the window. "You ever hear me talk about Willie? Guy who lives next door?"

A shiver danced up and down Lily's spine. "He's your best friend."

"Uh-huh. And he's Ricky's twin."

"Wow."

"Having him forgive me made all the difference."

"Makes sense." And it gave her food for thought.

She *would* feel better if she could confess what she'd done, already *did* feel better having told Long John. If she could tell Carson...

"Something to notice," Long John said. "You listened to me tell you the thing that, to me, is the most awful failing of my life. And you're still sittin' here. You didn't run off thinking I was a horrible person."

"No, of course not!" Lily studied him. "You had to make a terrible choice, and you did the best you could."

"Same goes for you, too," he said. "Are you supposed to never argue with anyone, just do what everyone says, on the chance that they might go self-destructive on you?"

"Noooo," she said cautiously.

He leaned forward, sipped some more tea. "And yes, we're our brothers' keepers, but we can't stop them from taking any risk. My buddy, he bucked orders by heading into that swamp. I couldn't stop him from doing that. Willie says he was always reckless that way."

She nodded. When she looked out the window, she saw that the sunset was turning the tops of the mountains to red flame. "I should go," she said, collecting their empty teacups and putting them over on the dish drainer.

"You think about what I've said now."

She shrugged into her coat. "I will." Impulsively, she leaned over and kissed the old man's dry, bristly cheek. "Thank you for helping me think it through."

As tears came to her eyes, she hurried out of the cabin with Bella.

She'd never known her grandfather, and certainly her father hadn't been a helpful influence. But Long John, today, felt like the grandfather she'd never had.

Not only that, but his words had lit a fire in her.

Tomorrow, she needed to tell Carson the truth about Pam.

The next afternoon, Carson was washing lunch dishes when there was a knock on the door. He dried his hands and glanced out the window.

Lily. Warmth spread through his chest and he walked double time to the door. Opened it and felt his mouth curve into an automatic smile.

"Hi," she said, her voice tentative. "Can I come in a minute?"

"Sure!" He beckoned her in. "The girls are working on some mysterious project up in the loft, and I'm all alone down here."

Had that sounded pathetic?

No, because she smiled back at him—nervously, true, but it was still a smile. "That's good," she said. "I wanted to talk to you about something."

"If you're worried about Sunny and the dog bite, she's fine," he said. "She had a dream where she was a little dog fighting with a big dog—"

"Oh, no! That sounds scary."

Carson laughed. "Not for Sunny. The little dog got the big dog a leash and took him for a walk, and then they became best friends." He grinned, remembering Sunny recounting the dream. "I don't actually know how much of it was a dream and how much an embellishment, but it seemed to make her feel better."

"It *was* my dream!" Sunny called from the loft. "Hi, Miss Lily."

"Hi, sweetie," Lily said, and they both smiled up at the rosy face that peeked over the loft railing.

"I can't come down because we're doing something *very important*."

"Come on, Sunny!" Skye called from the back of the loft area. Skye was his responsible one, always keeping her twin on task. He hoped that would translate into schoolwork when they got older.

"You can see it later, Miss Lily," Sunny promised. "But it's a secret from Daddy." Then she disappeared and her footsteps clattered across the floor above them.

Carson reached to help Lily take off her coat, chuckling. "They've been whispering and working for the past couple of hours. I think it's a late Christmas present. Come on, let me get you some coffee."

"That sounds good." She followed him into the kitchen area and leaned one hip against the counter.

She looked so pretty in slim-fitting jeans, a sweater and a vest. Outdoorsy, makeup-free, a natural beauty.

He wanted to talk more to her, learn about her. After his conversation with Long John, he was feeling increasingly certain that he wanted to get to know her better. And more hopeful that something might come of it.

"How's Bella?" he asked instead of leading with something deeper right away. Lily was skittish, like a wild animal. He had to approach getting closer in the right way, the slow way.

"She's doing fine. I'd like to think she feels bad

about what happened with Sunny, but truth to tell, I think she's forgotten all about it." She sighed. "I scolded her all the way home, but she just looked up at me with her tongue hanging out."

Carson could picture it, the pretty young woman lecturing, the dog laughing up at her. "How's her recovery?"

"I think she's doing great. Jack, the vet, he's coming up to look at her tomorrow."

Jealousy pushed into Carson's consciousness. Of course Jack was coming up to check on Bella. Probably to check on Lily, too. Check *out* Lily.

And what was it about the gentle woman standing in his kitchen that brought out his caveman instincts? He wanted her for his own.

He carried their mugs of coffee to the table, put them down and pulled out a chair for her. "Listen, Lily," he said, "after you leave the cabins, where are you headed?"

"That's a good question." She kneaded her hands together. "I'm almost done with my degree, and I don't have any real ties aside from finishing that work."

"You have your aunt Penny, right here. Ever think about sticking around this area?" Carson felt heat climb up his neck. He had no right to ask her a question like that.

She didn't seem to take offense. "I do love it here," she said. "Esperanza Springs is a really nice town. I've liked everyone I've met here, and it's so pretty."

"Do you like the snow?"

"Mostly." She held out her boot, showing him how the sole was flapping loose. "I obviously need to get new boots, and I wouldn't mind a warmer coat, but I do like it. Listen, Carson—"

What kind of a jerk was he, letting her freeze like that? "Sit tight. I'm going to get you some slippers."

He climbed halfway up the ladder. "Coming up, girls," he said.

"No, Daddy, you can't!" they said together.

"Then throw me down my slippers, will you? And a pair of my big warm socks from my suitcase."

Little feet clattered, and then socks and slippers soared out of the loft, one slipper hitting him on the head.

"Now stay down there," Skye lectured from the top of the ladder. "We're not finished yet."

"Okay, okay." He backed down the ladder, collected the footwear and went into the bathroom to grab a thick bath towel. Then he knelt in front of Lily. "Give me your foot."

"Oh, no, it's okay, you shouldn't…"

He ignored her protest, took her foot into his hands and gently pulled off her broken boot.

Her feet were delicate, pink and cold. He wrapped the towel around her foot and rubbed it dry. His hands wanted to linger, make this into a full-blown foot massage, but he knew better. *Remember, skittish.* He pulled a sock over her foot and fitted the slipper onto it.

He glanced up at her face. Her cheeks were pink, and when their eyes met, she blushed more deeply.

Quickly, he repeated the treatment on the other foot, trying to keep his movements businesslike rather than romantic. As soon as he'd put the second sock and slipper on her, he put her damp boots and socks in front of the fire. He took a moment to arrange them carefully, so he could calm his own racing pulse.

He was less and less immune to this woman. Physically and emotionally, yes, but spiritually, too. He wanted to take care of her.

If he were honest with himself, he hadn't done the best job of serving Pam. He'd meant well, but he'd been a little selfish, too young to look at their life from her point of view.

Next time, he'd do better.

Serving Lily that way would be an honor and a joy.

He walked over to the table and sat. She met his eyes and then looked down at her coffee cup, but he'd seen the uneasiness on her face. Should he keep things impersonal or try to go deeper?

He went with his gut, touched her hand. "I was asking you about where you might settle for a reason, and I need to say it before I lose my nerve."

"Before you… Okaaaay." She took a sip of black coffee, watching him over the rim of the cup.

"If you were to stay around here awhile," he said, "would you consider going out with me?"

She set down her mug too hard, making coffee splash onto the table.

Automatically he grabbed a napkin and wiped it up. Then he met her eyes again, a sinking feeling inside.

She hadn't answered. She didn't want to go out with him and was figuring out how to say so.

No woman as pretty and talented as Lily would want to date a small-town pastor, tied down with a couple of demanding kids. Why would she, when she could date anyone she wanted to?

Jack DeMoise, for example?

"You don't have to answer that," he said quickly, scrubbing at the table with the soggy napkin. "I didn't mean to put you on the spot. Of course, you have other things to think about besides dating, especially since you're basically just here on vacation—"

She put a hand over his. "Carson."

The throaty sound of her voice sent a heat wave through him, despite the cold day. Man, he had it bad. He was probably showing that, too, by the way he was acting. And he knew, had counseled his parishioners in job-hunting or dating situations, that desperation was never appealing.

Her hand was still on top of his, and he looked up to meet her eyes.

"I like you a lot, Carson," she said, "and I like your girls a lot, too."

"But…" He tried to say it in a joking way, to soften the blow to his own ego. "There's always a 'but.'"

"Yes, there is," she said, looking at him seriously. "There's something I need to tell you first."

Chapter Eleven

Lily looked at Carson's dear face and tried to hold on to her reasons for telling him the truth.

She thought of Long John, who'd confessed his wartime sin and not only felt more peace, but had built a lifelong friendship with the person he'd confessed to.

Carson was offering a relationship, or at least the start of one. But a relationship without honesty would never work.

And she was starting to think that maybe, just maybe, she was worthy of love and could be loved. That she could build a community and a life in this cold but warmhearted place.

"It's about Pam," she blurted out before she could lose courage. But then she did lose courage, her heart pounding hard and fast like some tribal drum.

He smiled at her, his face gentle. "What about Pam?"

She drew in a shaky breath. "It's...not good."

He reached out and covered her hand with his. "Lily, whatever Pam did, it's no reflection on you."

But he didn't know what she'd done to cause Pam's death. "Carson, shortly before Pam died, I—"

"Miss Lily, Miss Lily, come and see!"

"And help us!"

Carson squeezed her hand. "Just a minute, girls," he called upstairs.

"Daddy, you can't come! You stay down there!"

"Come on, Miss Lily, you have to help us now!"

The girls' voices were loud. She looked at Carson.

She should get this confession out of the way. She'd started; she'd come this far.

But no way could they have a real conversation with the girls clamoring for attention upstairs.

"Go ahead," he said. "We can talk later. Maybe tonight." His voice was full of promise.

Oh, how she hoped that promise would remain once he'd heard what she had to say.

She smiled and walked by him and climbed the ladder to the loft. Carson stood behind her, always protective, there to catch her if she fell.

His kind, compassionate nature made her hope that he'd be able to understand what had happened. He'd learned forgiveness, had modeled it, in his years of being a pastor. She hoped it would apply to her.

She reached the top, and immediately the twins rushed to her. "Miss Lily, come see what we made Daddy!"

She went over to the bed, where the girls had laid out a large poster board. On it was a dizzying array of photographs and drawings, ribbons and medals and...

Medals?

Then she saw the headline: Our Mommy.

She looked more closely at the photographs. Pam was in every one.

"Wow, this is…really something." Lily swallowed hard at all the images of her friend: with the girls, in her uniform, with Carson.

"It's for Daddy," Skye explained. "'Cuz we listened to Mr. Long John saying he needed to get over her."

"Deal with her," Sunny corrected.

"And face the truth about her."

"And then he could move on, and maybe we could get a new mommy!"

"Oh." As Lily's legs went jelly-ish, she sat down on the bed beside the poster to look at it more closely and try to collect herself, getting a little wet paint on her wrist in the process.

There, in the center of the poster board, was an official-looking paper. She leaned forward to read it.

DISCHARGE UNDER OTHER THAN HONORABLE CONDITIONS.

Her heart thumped painfully. "Where did you get this?" she asked the twins, who'd started arguing over who had to clean up some spilled glue.

"Oh! That came in the mail," Skye said.

"So we hid it away with all our Mommy stuff before Daddy could see."

"Because sometimes papers that look like that make Daddy sad."

Lily swallowed. "How long ago?"

The twins looked at each other. "A long time," Sunny said.

"Maybe when we were five," Skye added.

"We have a big box of Mommy things. We stopped at home for it yesterday, when we went to town for the birthday party, 'cause we knew then we wanted to make this."

"And we sneaked it outside. We told Daddy it was toys." Skye frowned. "Do you think that was a bad lie, Miss Lily?"

"What?" Lily had been barely paying attention to the twins' explanations, because she was trying to understand the situation and figure out what to do.

The twins couldn't read the dishonorable discharge, obviously; it was full of military jargon, words too big for them to understand at six. They thought the paper was a good thing.

Carson certainly wouldn't.

Right after Pam had died, Lily had talked to a superior officer about whether Pam's discharge would have been effective immediately, such that her family wouldn't get military benefits. They'd figured out that since Pam's death had come only hours after the discharge meeting, it wouldn't have been official yet.

In her limited conversations with Carson, Lily had realized that he didn't know about the discharge. She'd guessed, had hoped, it had never been processed.

But here was the paperwork to suggest otherwise. One of those mix-ups that tended to happen in a giant, form-heavy organization like the US Army.

If, as she suspected, Carson didn't know, then there was a whole layer of information he'd need to come to terms with, in addition to the way Pam had died.

He wouldn't like it, not any of it, not one bit.

"Can you help us carry it down to Daddy?" Sunny asked. "It's still a little wet from glue, and we don't want to mess it up."

Could she do that? Deliver the bad news with her own hands?

"Girls, I'm not sure this paper will make Daddy happy," she said, pointing at the discharge letter.

Their faces fell. "Why not?"

How did you explain something like that? "It's complicated," she said weakly.

"Should we take it off?" Skye asked.

"If we take it off, it'll rip, because we put that on first," Sunny said. "Why do you think it won't make Daddy happy, Miss Lily?"

The sound of footsteps on the ladder forestalled her from any impossible answer she might make. "What's going on up here?" Carson boomed in a comical, read-aloud voice.

"Daddy, you can't look! Because Miss Lily thinks you won't like it!"

"I think he will," Sunny said stubbornly. "And Miss Lily is mean for saying he won't."

Carson's head and then the rest of him appeared at the top of the ladder.

Lily looked at the twins' faces and then at Carson's. Whatever she said, whatever she did, someone would get hurt.

"I think your daddy will love your gift because of the work you did," she said, looking at Carson, trying to telegraph to him that he needed to school his reaction. "Even if some of the things on it are a surprise, or make him a little sad, he knows you girls are trying to make him happy."

"And get him ready for our new mommy," added the irrepressible Sunny.

"Sunny. I told you not to talk about that." Carson

climbed the rest of the way up the ladder and walked over, ducking his head to avoid hitting it on the loft's slanted roof.

"Ta-daaah!" Sunny cried, and after a second's pause, Skye echoed her twin's words.

A smile curved Carson's lips as he looked down at the poster, and Lily tried to freeze that smile in her head, to remember how kind and happy he looked.

She had a feeling she wasn't going to see that expression on his face again.

And sure enough, his smile faded as he saw the topic of the poster. "Our Mommy," he read aloud, and looked from one twin to the other.

"Because you have to face it," Skye explained. "Mr. Long John said."

He put an arm around her shoulders, and then Sunny came to his other side, and all three bent over the poster.

"See, there's the time she took us to the playground," Sunny said.

"And here's when she cooked us a birthday cake."

The girls prattled on, pointing out various photos with an emphasis on themselves.

Lily saw the moment when Carson read the military paper, because his shoulders stiffened. "Other than honorable… Where did you girls get this paper?"

Skye glanced nervously back at Lily. "Does it make you too sad, Daddy?"

"Where did you get it?" he repeated.

"It came in an envelope, and we hid it," Skye said, her voice shaky. "But not to be bad. We just thought papers with that picture—" she pointed at the official army insignia "—sometimes they make you sad. We didn't know you needed to *face* it."

He nodded and patted Skye's shoulder, his lips pressed tightly together. Then he looked up at Lily. "Did you know about this?"

She looked into his dear, hurt eyes and nodded. "About the discharge, yes." The last word came out in a croak, pushing through her tight throat.

He opened his mouth to ask another question and then looked down at his daughters, both watching him, both faces concerned, Skye's scrunching up toward tears.

"I love the thoughtfulness and caring you put into this gift," he said, his voice a little husky. He knelt down and pulled them both close.

His wrinkled forehead and downturned mouth, as he looked at Lily over the heads of the little girls, told another story.

He was confused and upset, of course. He was learning something terrible about his wife.

It still wasn't the worst thing, though.

He stood and clapped his hands. "I'm going to take this downstairs where the light is better, so I can look at it more," he said. "And then I'm going to take you girls over to see Long John, because he told me Rockette is getting lonely."

"Yes!" Sunny pumped her fist.

"Are you mad at us, Daddy?" Skye asked.

He put his hands on Skye's shoulders. "No, of course not. It's a very caring gift." He kissed her forehead. "Now, clean up a little and then we'll hurry over to Long John's."

"Okay!" Skye rushed over to where Sunny was already stuffing paper scraps into a trash can.

Carson looked at Lily. "I need to talk to you."

She couldn't tell him the truth. But now she couldn't *not* tell him.

Lily watched Carson walk up the road toward Long John's cabin, a twin on either side, holding their hands. It was a picture of idyllic family happiness, etched against the blue sky and the mountains.

But Lily knew Carson well enough to see the unusual rigidity of his shoulders.

He'd invented that planned visit to Long John. He was going to come back here and demand to know everything.

It would start with the discharge and go on from there. And when he found out the whole truth about Pam, he'd be furious at Lily for not telling him right away. Worse, he'd be devastated.

She shouldn't have kept the secret, but how could she not when the whole thing was her fault in the first place?

She'd never been able to navigate the complicated waters of her parents' relationship, keeping them both happy and providing the buffer they needed, being there when they wanted her and away when they didn't.

She'd been a difficult child, as her mother had so often told her.

This past week, immersed in the mountains and in the culture of Esperanza Springs, she'd started to feel different about herself. The acceptance from Carson, the uncomplicated affection of the twins, the joy of a Christmas that had started out lonely and ended up warmly connected—all of it had begun to work a change in Lily. New birth, new life, fitting for the Christmas season.

But it had all been a facade, because she *wasn't* reborn. She was the same old messed-up Lily.

Only now the consequences were devastating, and every minute brought closer the time when more people would be hurt.

How could she cut the pain? How could she make it at least a little better for Carson and the girls?

She squinted out the window. The little family was almost to Long John's place now, two colorful specks with a tall, dark figure between them.

In less than a week, they'd come to mean so much to her. The trusting little girls, the funny, warm pastor… the way they'd accepted her into their circle, cared for her…it was all she'd ever wanted.

Maybe she could tell Carson the truth in a way that would make him understand. Maybe she could explain part, but not all, of the details of Pam's death, sparing him the worst of it.

But knowing Carson, how observant he was, he'd know there was more and would insist on the truth. And it would break his heart.

Did she have the right to break his heart?

Did she have the strength to do what was necessary to avoid breaking it? To sacrifice her own happiness for his?

The three figures had disappeared from sight. They had to be inside Long John's cabin by now, which meant that Carson would be striding back any minute, insisting on an explanation that would devastate him.

She rushed to the kitchen table, found pen and paper, and composed a note. Prayed a quick apology for lying, and hoped she was right that the damage to Carson and the girls would be minimized by the act.

Then she ran to her cabin, threw her belongings into her suitcase willy-nilly and carried them to the door.

Bella whined, looking mournfully up at her, seeming to know something momentous was going on.

The sight of the dog's concerned face released the tears Lily had been fighting off. She knelt and wrapped her arms around the big, bony dog. Bella licked at her cheeks, gently wiping her tears.

Oh, how she wanted to take Bella with her. But the dog was too old and frail to make the trip, especially since Lily's destination was uncertain. Better to leave her here in the warm cabin as she'd originally planned.

She'd asked it in the note, and so Carson would take care of Bella. Lily trusted him for that.

Her throat impossibly tight, she picked up her bag, slipped out the cabin door and closed it behind her. Minutes later she'd started down toward the highway, wiping tears with the backs of her cold hands.

Heading to Arizona, simply because she had nowhere else to go.

Carson marched back to the cabin at military pace, almost a jog, fueled by anger and confusion and pain.

Pam had been other-than-honorably discharged?

He didn't want to believe it. It didn't make sense. He and the girls had received the survivors' benefits. Nobody at the VA had said anything about a discharge, let alone a dishonorable one.

Halfway there, his steps slowed.

Unpleasant facts were pushing their way into his consciousness. The things a couple of friends had said about Pam's behavior overseas. Her impatient mentions, during Skype calls, of meetings with commanding officers, of mix-ups about whether she was allowed to go off base or not.

Pam's thrill-seeking personality, the behaviors that had gotten her in trouble stateside, had been at odds with the discipline required of soldiers.

Lately, he'd realized how far from perfect Pam had been as a wife and mother. She'd had serious flaws. But if she'd also gotten into trouble as a soldier—trouble significant enough to lead to a bad discharge—was there nothing good to say about her?

The pedestal on which he'd placed his beautiful wife, already cracked, began to crumble into pieces.

Shying away from those thoughts, his mind settled on Lily. On her sad, knowing face as she'd admitted that, yes, she knew about the discharge.

No wonder Lily hadn't wanted to talk about Pam! She'd been hiding huge pieces of the puzzle. Why, he couldn't understand. What did Lily stand to gain from lying to him?

A light snow was starting to fall. He looked ahead toward his cabin and suddenly was filled with a bursting desire to know the truth, the whole truth, about Pam's last days and her death. He practically ran up the steps, flung open the door. "Lily! I want some answers."

But she was nowhere in sight.

He hunted quickly through the main room and then climbed the ladder to the loft. No Lily.

So she'd gone back to her place.

No way was he letting this slide. He'd go over there, right now.

On his way to the door, he looked down at the table and saw a paper that didn't belong. Picked up the hastily scrawled note.

Carson, I'm sorry, but I've decided to leave the area. The isolation and lack of cultural resources bother me, and I feel that you and the girls are getting too attached to me when I'll never be able to return the feelings.
Regards,
Lily
PS: Could you please put Bella back in the kennel for me?

He stared at the cold note and tried to reconcile it with the woman he knew.

No "give my best to the girls"?

"Regards"?

It didn't sound anything like Lily, but it was undeniably her handwriting.

Maybe he hadn't known her at all. His legs suddenly weak, he shrugged out of his coat and sat down. Lily's complaint about the region was far too familiar. It was what Pam had said at first, before the real problem surfaced: *he* was too boring, too tame, too upright.

But being boring has its strong points, Pam. Like, you don't get in so much trouble that you're dishonorably discharged from the armed forces.

He couldn't figure it out. Was Lily just trying to escape a difficult conversation, or did she feel the same way Pam did?

He looked out the window, his stomach knotting. He tried to focus on the beautiful faraway mountains that had been here before his petty human problems and would be here after. Tried to connect with the divine force that had made them.

Why, God, why?

He'd started to think Lily's coming here showed God's hand, that the Lord had brought them together for a reason, healing for both of them and for the girls. The Christmas Eve celebration in Long John's cabin, when she'd helped the girls decorate those cookies that were even now blaring their colors and sparkles from a plate on the table. The way she'd smiled as she'd photographed his little family, as they'd watched the girls speed down the hill on their sled. The compassion in her eyes as she'd leaned over an injured dog.

It all flashed before him and was gone in an instant, replaced by the cold, almost mocking words of the note before him.

He read it again, and this time he realized something else.

She'd said she was leaving. Was she already gone?

He half stood and looked over toward her cabin. Through the snowflakes, he couldn't see any lights.

Her car was gone.

She was gone.

Chapter Twelve

Lily clenched the steering wheel and peered through the snow, making her way down the lonely mountain road toward the busier highway that would take her home.

Or what passed for home. Funny, even though she'd spent only a week in Colorado, she had the feeling she was *leaving* home.

The car slid a little on its nearly bald tires, tires that had seemed perfectly fine in the desert Southwest. She sucked in a gasp and tapped the brakes lightly, and the car came back into line.

Had she made a terrible mistake, writing that awful letter to Carson? Not just abandoning him and the girls and poor sweet Bella, but doing it in a cold, uncaring way that would definitely sever any relationship that was left between them?

No, because knowing Carson, knowing the way he cared for others, he'd come after her if she didn't cut him off completely. Not because he loved her, specifically, but because he wouldn't want any person to be at risk in snow like this.

He loved people, all people. It was his nature, and it wasn't fake and insincere like some men, even pastors, that she'd met in the past. His generosity and concern for others went heart-deep.

But he wouldn't be able to love her, not after what she'd done. She'd seen the look of betrayal on his face, just hearing about the discharge. Well, what would happen if he learned the whole truth?

He'd put part of the blame on himself, of course, and that would make him miserable.

But he'd also blame Lily, and rightly so.

Pam had certainly laid the blame at Lily's feet. *Some friend you are! You threw me to the wolves! It's all your fault!*

The horrible memories came rushing back and she fumbled for tissues. She swiped at her eyes and then grabbed a half-frozen water bottle and took a drink, trying to calm herself, to force the ugly pictures out of her mind. She couldn't allow herself an emotional breakdown now, on a snow-covered road.

She needed to think of something else.

She noticed the paint smear on her wrist, and immediately her mind was cast back to the twins' eager, adorable faces.

The sob that rose from her chest made her buck forward, and instinctively she hit the brake to slow down, making the car fishtail.

Just like it had the first morning she'd been here, when the twins had come running down to offer six-year-old advice and assistance.

They were so dear. Such sweet, good little girls. Fun-loving, with a hint of Pam's mischief and a bigger dose of Carson's kindness.

She'd never see them again.

She swallowed hard, clenched her jaw. *Get it together; you can do this.*

For the tiniest second, she caught a glimpse of Pam's despair. When you felt like you'd lost everything, when it seemed that no one cared, when to go on living meant a bucketload of pain and no one to help you deal with it, when you'd hurt the ones you loved... Yeah. It made at least a little sense.

Lily glanced toward the dropoff on the left side of the road.

No. She sucked in deep breaths and focused on the narrow, slippery highway in front of her. She couldn't let herself wreck and freeze and die out here.

She had to believe God had some kind of a plan, even if it felt as blurry and hazy as the low-visibility air in front of her.

She gripped the steering wheel tighter, navigated around a curve. Lost traction.

Her car skidded sideways, and she tried to steer into it, braking as lightly as she could, hands suddenly sweaty on the wheel.

There was a jolt, and then the car did a sickening nosedive, bumping Lily's head forward to the steering wheel, back against the headrest and then forward again.

Help, Father!

Carson paced his cabin, trying not to look at the note he'd let flutter to the floor. Trying to pray.

He should probably just go get the girls. Oh, they were fine; Long John had said they could stay as long as he needed, and they'd been settled in to watch a gentle nature show while cuddling with Rockette.

It was Carson who needed them this time, not the reverse. So that he could focus on what he was good at: being a dad. Forget about Lily.

Maybe he should go after her.

The inaudible nudge felt completely familiar to Carson. He'd experienced it before.

She doesn't want me, Father. She made that perfectly clear. He even gestured at the note on the floor, as if God needed to be reminded of the truth.

She'd sure acted friendly, though. She'd seemed to like Carson for who he was, had seemed content with small-town life, had seemed to love hanging around the cabin with him and the girls.

How did her note fit in with that? Had her contentment and enjoyment all been fake?

He slammed a fist against the wall. She'd deliberately misled him, which was bad enough, but she'd also gotten his girls involved. Put their hearts at risk, when she of all people should understand how vulnerable they were, having lost their mother.

They'd be devastated when they learned that Lily had gone away.

He should never have let them get close to her. *He* shouldn't have gotten close to her. She wasn't worth it.

She wasn't.

There came that inner nudge to go after her, again.

"No!" He shouted the word aloud, then felt like an idiot. Anyone looking in at him would think he was flat-out crazy.

He knew the truth, though. His craziness didn't consist of walking around by himself yelling and hitting things. It consisted of getting involved with the wrong woman, not just once, but twice.

A gust of wind whipped around the cabin, making a lonely whistle.

Against his will, an image of Lily driving alone through the winter weather formed itself in his mind. She didn't even have good boots, and she wasn't comfortable driving in these slippery, whiteout conditions. If she went off the road…

Carson blew out a sigh and looked out through the increasingly heavy snow toward the spot where Lily's car should be.

Even if she'd had the skill and comfort level, she wasn't equipped for snow driving. Her vehicle wasn't made for it. She probably didn't even have a blanket in the car, let alone a shovel, gravel, water, snacks. Things any rural Coloradoan wouldn't need to be told to carry along, but she wasn't from around here.

And night would fall early at this, the darkest time of the year.

Arguing with himself, he started coffee brewing. Then he texted Long John, got back into his coat and boots, and stuffed a blanket, extra socks and mittens into a backpack.

He poured the fresh coffee into his big thermos and stuck that in the pack, too. If he *did* catch up with her, she'd need it. She loved her coffee.

Minutes later he was on the slick, icy road, making his way carefully around the bends. No other vehicles in sight. People knew better than to drive in weather like this.

Lily didn't, though. And while he'd started his rescue trip berating himself as a fool, now he was glad he'd come.

She'd withheld information, made him angry. But she was a fellow human being who needed help, and for whatever reason, God had put him in a position to help her.

He was steering around a particularly tight curve when he saw the back end of her car, poking up out of the roadside ditch. His heart gave a great leap. He found the next safe spot to pull off, got out with his backpack of equipment and rushed to her car.

She wasn't in it.

Lily's face stung with the cold, and her feet were blocks of ice.

Had she made a mistake, leaving the car?

Of course you did, came a familiar, critical voice from inside. *Always causing problems. Never in the right place. Making trouble for everyone.*

She rolled her eyes. *Thanks, Mom. I needed that.*

Thing was, her winter wandering might *not* cause trouble for anyone. Who would know she was gone, who would care, now that she'd cut off her ties with Carson and the twins?

But Aunt Penny would care. Long John would care. If she thought about it, a few friends from her university program would care, and a couple of army buddies. Even her father would care, if he were sober enough to be aware of her absence.

Would anyone get to her in time, though, if she were reported missing? By the time her car was found, she'd likely be a stick of ice.

All the more important that she reach her destination. She'd remembered this area from her drive up here, and she knew there was a small cluster of cabins on a lake visible from the road. She'd thought it looked so cute and welcoming.

If she could just reach those cabins, she could find help or at least shelter. And that would be better than staying in her less-than-airtight, not-that-reliable car that had quit running and wouldn't turn on again.

The trouble was, she could barely see through the blizzard-like whiteness, and it was getting increasingly difficult to trudge through the snow in her loose-soled boots. Twice, she'd fallen, and now she fell again. This time, it was harder to get back up.

She tried to feel God's presence. Never had she needed Him so badly. For emotional survival and physical, too.

Was that a building ahead? She got to her feet and squinted toward the dark shape, stomping her feet and rubbing her hands together. When she realized it was one of the cabins, she ran toward it, slipping and stumbling in the snow, praying for a friendly reception.

But when she got there, the cabin was cold and empty.

Carson strode as fast as safely possible in the shin-deep snow. The path Lily had broken was filling in quickly, and he was terrified of losing her.

What kind of a person would leave the warmth of her car and strike out across a windy field in a snowstorm? Didn't Lily know she was putting herself, as well as anyone searching for her, at risk?

He tried to work up more righteous anger. Inconsiderate, that was what it was. She was thinking of herself and not of others. Maybe that offhanded note she'd left on the table represented the real her, and if so, once he found her, he'd take her to the nearest airport and deposit her there, no problem.

Yeah, right.

He plunged forward through the deepening snow and then realized he was off her path. Panic gripped him as he scanned the surrounding whiteness, but he floundered back and picked up her trail again. Where was she going? Was she headed to that abandoned miners' camp that served as an unofficial shelter for local hunters?

What would she do once there?

He wished he didn't care about her so much. But he did. The thought of her out here alone—or encountering a sketchy, drunk group of hunters—made him move faster.

He had to admit the truth; he'd fallen hard for her.

And as he thought about Lily, as memories of their short-but-intense time together flashed through his mind, he knew she'd felt something, too.

She'd certainly seemed to care. To enjoy what he had to offer, and he *did* have something to offer. He wasn't an urban sophisticate or an international playboy, but those types wouldn't suit Lily. She was country to the core.

And if he found her, he was going to tell her so.

He made out the shape of the cabins through the sideways-blowing snow and was relieved to see her footprints led in that direction. If she'd gotten inside to safety, she'd be all right. Cold, wet, uncomfortable, but all right.

And once he got her thawed out, he'd demand an

explanation of what she knew about Pam and why she'd hidden the truth.

Suddenly, a familiar fragrance met his nostrils.

Woodsmoke? Here?

And there was light inside one of the cabins. Maybe someone was staying here after all, and he could only hope that, if it were a hunter, it was a friendly rather than a dangerous one.

He practically ran the last few steps to the door, pounded on it and then flung it open.

And there, sitting cross-legged in front of a roaring fire, was Lily. Relief overwhelmed him, and he automatically looked skyward, breathing out a silent "thank you."

"Carson!" She sounded shocked. "How…how on earth did you find me? And why…" She trailed off, her head cocked to one side.

He scanned the cabin—rudimentary, dirty and empty but for her—and then stood in the doorway, staring at her. "You're fine!" he accused at last. Which was a ridiculous thing to say, and the annoyance he felt was ridiculous, too. But he'd fought his way here through the storm, thinking she'd be desperate and half-dead.

Apparently, she wasn't as helpless as he'd thought her to be.

She rose gracefully to her feet. "I'm not *fine,*" she said. "I'm still thawing out. And it looks like you need to do the same."

"How'd you build a fire?"

She gave him a tentative smile. "There were matches and wood here. I was a Girl Scout for a couple of years. Could you close the door?"

He pulled it shut behind him, and the roar of the wind quieted.

He shucked his coat and knelt beside his backpack. "We have some talking to do," he said. "And knowing you, it'll go better if you have coffee."

"You brought *coffee*?"

The delight in her voice just about undid him. He liked bringing pleasure to this complicated woman.

He pulled it out and poured her a steaming cup. When he offered it to her, her hands, pink and cold-looking, curled around it. "Thank you," she said. "Oh, Carson, I shouldn't have run away."

He busied himself with pulling the remaining supplies out of the backpack. "That note," he said.

"Was a lie," she admitted immediately. "The first I've ever told you, and I'm sorry."

"Why did you do it, Lily? Why would you say those things if they weren't true?"

She took a sip of coffee. "I was trying to protect myself from your anger," she said. "And trying to figure out how to tell you something."

"What kind of something?" he asked, although he had a pretty good guess.

"The truth about what happened to Pam." She bit her lip. "You're going to hate me for it, Carson, so I'd just about decided to write it in a letter. But now that you're here…" She swallowed convulsively. "Now that you're here, I'll have to tell you in person."

The firmness in her voice and resolution in her eyes took him aback, almost as much as the cozy fire had done. Now that she was willing to talk, Carson felt an odd reluctance to hear what she had to say.

She drew him toward the fire. "Sit down," she said,

indicating the floor beside her. "What I'm going to tell you, you'll want to be sitting down."

Something about her tone made the hairs on the back of his neck rise, and he paused in the act of sitting on the dirty, rough-hewn floor. "We should get out of this storm. You can tell me later."

"I'll lose my courage," she said. "It's not going to get that much worse in half an hour. Please, just listen."

He sank the rest of the way to the floor. "Okay. So first off, why didn't you tell me about Pam's dishonorable discharge?"

She closed her eyes for a moment, then opened them again and looked straight at him. "It wasn't even supposed to happen," she said. "When Pam…was killed, I knew she'd just been meeting with our CO about her status. They said in that situation, since the meeting had only happened that day, they'd let it go. She died before being officially discharged, so it kind of didn't count." She shook her head. "But you know what a big bureaucracy the army is. Some paperwork must have gotten started and nobody canceled it."

He had to force himself to stay calm, not to jump up and yell at her. "You had all these discussions with other people about Pam's death, and you couldn't tell the details to me, her husband?"

"There's a reason—"

"I don't get it, Lily. I thought you were a good person. Thought you were starting to care for me and the girls, but how could you care when you kept this big—this *huge*—piece of information from us?"

She blew out a breath, glanced up at the ceiling and then leaned forward. "Look, I'm going to tell you exactly what happened," she said. "I think you'll understand then why I didn't want you to know."

A sick feeling formed in the center of Carson's chest, and again he had the desire to get out of there, not to hear what she had to say. He even looked out the small cabin's window, saw the growing darkness and opened his mouth to tell her they should leave instead.

But she started speaking rapidly. "You heard about some of Pam's run-ins with military authority, right? How she kept getting in trouble, was confined to base, stuff like that?"

"Some of it." He was ashamed to admit that he didn't know much about that, just a few hints he'd picked up. It was one of many indications that his relationship with his wife hadn't been the best.

But if she was going to be honest, he would, too. "Truth is," he said, "Pam didn't like to tell me about things like that, because she knew I'd scold her. I wanted her to be careful and take care of herself, not run around. And I was jealous. I could guess she wasn't doing those kinds of things alone."

Lily cocked her head to one side. "She wasn't unfaithful that I knew of, Carson. That wasn't the problem."

Something tight he'd been carrying in his chest loosened up. "Then what happened?"

"She was out looking for adventure, excitement. She said army life was boring."

That sounded like Pam.

"And she was doing a lot of drinking. Even some drugs."

"She was pregnant!"

"I didn't know that. Maybe she cut down when she found out."

"Don't placate me!" He'd kind of known Pam didn't want the baby, but this sealed it.

She looked at him with misery in her eyes. "Things came to a head a couple of weeks before, well, before she died. Investigators came and talked to me about what I'd observed, as her roommate, and…I told the truth."

"What do you mean?"

"I told them the things that led to her dishonorable discharge." She bit her lip. "Showed them her stash of drugs, gave them her diary. Carson, I caused her death."

"What do you mean?" He imagined Pam's sense of betrayal at having her secrets revealed. Lily had been a close friend. Still, to say that had caused her death seemed extreme.

And wait: Pam had had a stash of drugs?

"She was furious, because the evidence from me was part of what led to her discharge." Her hands were twisting together. "I've rethought my conversation with the investigators over and over, and I can't figure out what I could have done differently. She was going out high, see, and of course she had her weapon. It was so dangerous, and she wouldn't listen to me. I'd thought about reporting her myself, but before I could make that decision, the investigators came to me."

Carson's stomach twisted to think of Pam that way. Desperate enough to do drugs; cavalier enough to put other soldiers—and her baby—at risk.

Deceptive enough to hide the whole situation from

her husband. All those "I'm fine" video calls, her cheerful smiles and jokes and songs for the girls.

All of it a lie, apparently.

"I'm so sorry, Carson. I never wanted to get her in trouble."

He looked at her distressed face and believed her. "It sounds like you did what you had to do."

Lily swallowed. "On the day she died, Pam came running out to the guard hut where I was working. She was furious, yelling and waving her arms around. She told me I'd betrayed her and was an awful friend. She was raving."

Carson nodded slowly. "I've seen her like that a few times. I just can't believe they let her leave a discharge meeting and go out on her own in that state."

"The whole base was crazy. Reports of suspicious vehicles everywhere had come up, real sudden. So after her board meeting they put a junior guy in charge of Pam."

Carson could imagine how that had played out. Pam's mixture of charm and determination, even her beauty, could have flummoxed an inexperienced soldier.

He looked back at Lily to see her eyes filling with tears. "She told me that I'd ruined her life," she choked out. "And then she opened the door of the hut and ran out into the road, just as a suspicious vehicle we'd been watching for all day came into view. We'd gotten warnings about this vehicle, and we were all yelling for her to come back and get down, but she refused. She just walked right into it."

"She must not have known."

Lily bit her lip. "She *did* know."

"But if she knew how dangerous it was, then…"

He trailed off as what she was hinting at pushed its way into his mind.

He looked at Lily, hoping she'd have another explanation.

"I'm sorry, Carson," she said, "but she did it on purpose. She ended her life on purpose."

"No." He was shaking his head, shaking the words away. "No, she wouldn't have done that."

"Right before she ran out of the hut, she handed me a note."

A great stone pushed down on him. "What kind of a note?"

She swallowed and didn't answer. "She put it in my hand and told me not to tell anyone, to keep that private at least, not to betray her again." She put her face into her hands and let out one gulping sob. Wiped her eyes on her sleeve and looked up. "Then she went out into the line of fire."

Everything in him pushed away the notion. "You must have misunderstood. She wouldn't do that. Not to the girls. And she…" He couldn't go on, but he couldn't stop the thoughts and realizations, either.

She'd been pregnant with their third child. "I can't believe that."

"I have the note."

He stared. "You have a note and you didn't tell me?"

She nodded. And then, unbelievably, she fumbled in her coat, pulled out her wallet and opened it. Extracted a small piece of paper and handed it to him.

Tears were running down her face, but he couldn't spare sympathy for her. Instead, he read it aloud. Just three lines.

You destroyed my life.
I can't face what they're going to do to me.
This is on you.

Pam had purposely walked into enemy fire. She'd destroyed their baby. As well as abandoned Carson and, worse, the girls.

He let his head sink down into his hands. The thoughts, the words were too much.

His whole world was darkness.

Chapter Thirteen

Lily watched Carson's shoulders hunch in, his head resting in his hands. She couldn't see his face, but she knew that he was distraught beyond words.

He'd hate her forever for this.

"I'm so sorry," she said, wanting to blurt out the words before he shut down entirely. "If I hadn't told the investigators all I did, or if I'd responded better when she came to the guard hut so upset…"

But he wasn't listening. He didn't need to hear her details or apologies. He was devastated, just as she'd known he would be.

If only she'd never come here, he would never have had to know the painful truth.

Why couldn't she have had the strength to turn him away when he'd arrived here tonight? Why had her heart leaped with happiness? Selfish, selfish, selfish.

She went over and sat beside him. Not touching him, but shoulder to shoulder. She looked into the fire, now dying down a little, and tried to talk to God.

By the time Carson stirred from his slumped position, the sky outside had darkened. Lily had finished her coffee, and she'd found the blanket in his pack to drape around his shoulders. She'd wandered the cabin and found a spot where there was intermittent cell phone reception, and had texted Long John that Carson was safe and with her.

She was poking at the fire, trying to get a few last flames out of it, when she felt him looking at her.

His face was sunken. He looked like he'd aged twenty years.

Oh, Pam. "I'm sorry I couldn't prevent her death. So sorry. And I'm sorry I kept the truth from you." Inadequate words, obviously, but the best she could do.

She felt hammered by the events of the day. And by the crushing sensation that she'd let Pam down, let Carson down, let the twins down.

And the pain in Carson's face gutted her. Hurt her as if it were her own.

He pushed himself to his feet, his motions jerky, and studied her. "I've got to get out of here."

She stood, too. "Of course."

"I'll take you wherever you need to go, as long as it's away from the ranch and me and the girls."

She'd expected this, but his words still cut like blades.

"Can I drive you somewhere?" His voice sounded like a parody of the kind, helpful pastor.

Drive her somewhere. Help her to leave.

She'd been headed south with the idea of driving back to Phoenix, but that wasn't going to work, not with her car in a ditch.

And yet she couldn't go back to the cabin.

She had to get far, far away, both for her own sake and for Carson's.

A plan formulated in her mind, and she spoke up as soon as she thought of it. "Could you take me to the bus station in Trinidad?"

"You want to take a Greyhound bus in a snow-storm?"

No, she didn't want to, it was killing her, but if she was going, she had to do it fast. "If you can't, it's okay. I'm sure I can get someone in Esperanza Springs to take me, if you can run me back there."

"I'll take you." He stood abruptly. "But we should get moving. The roads won't get any better. What are you doing about your car?"

His businesslike attitude hurt, but it was for the best. "I think I can call someone to tow it. Maybe even donate it, if it can't be fixed."

"Sure." He nodded. "I'll put out the last of this fire. Gather your things." His voice was stern, impersonal.

She couldn't bear for him to be like this, couldn't bear for their connection to be entirely gone. "Did... did you get Bella back to the kennel?" The thought of the poor old dog had been hovering at the back of her mind. Bella didn't understand all this human drama; she just wanted a quiet place to rest and be loved.

Didn't they all.

"I haven't had time to move Bella," he said, still in that detached tone, "but I'll take care of it."

Don't be like that, she wanted to scream. *Be your old self with me.*

But that old self was gone. She'd killed it with her deceptions and mistakes.

She bundled up and then helped him haul in snow to make sure the fire was out.

"You ready?"

No. "Sure."

"I'll break a path. Walk behind me."

It was the most miserable walk of Lily's life. She followed Carson, never taking her eyes off him, trying to memorize the set of his shoulders, the slight hitch in his gait she'd never noticed before, maybe an old sports injury. The curl of hair that peeked out beneath his cap when he turned to check on her, make sure she was still there.

The hour-long ride to the little town of Trinidad was miserable, too. Carson turned on the radio, but it was mostly static. No good as a distraction. He drove expertly, not overly fast but not creeping along.

By the time they pulled into the small truck stop that housed the bus station in Trinidad, Lily already had her hand on the door handle. "You can just drop me off at the front door," she said.

"I can't just leave you here in the middle of nowhere," he said in a tone that brooked no reply. "I'll come in."

If he sat with her for the hours it would probably take for a bus to arrive, she wouldn't be able to bear it. And neither, from the looks of it, would he; he was just offering to stay because he was a protector and a gentleman to the core.

She made herself smile at him then, cool and impersonal. "I'll be fine, Carson," she said, even though the place, mostly deserted in the storm, made her nervous. "Don't give it a moment's thought." She jumped out and was reaching for her bag when he came around and pulled it out for her.

Now that it was really goodbye, Lily's courage

failed. She couldn't look at him, couldn't stop the tears that welled up in her eyes.

"Listen," he said gruffly. "I can take you back to the ranch. Give you time to think things through and figure out your next step, at least."

"No." She didn't dare return to the ranch. Didn't dare see the girls again. "Thanks for everything," she whispered, knowing her voice was barely audible over the lonely wind. "Tell…the twins…I love them."

It was all she could say. She couldn't look at his face. Instead, she grabbed her bag, gave his arm a quick squeeze and ran into the station.

As it turned out, she would have a long wait for the next bus south, but there was one going north in just three hours. She looked at the map given to her by a sleepy clerk and traced the routes with her finger, tears blurring her vision.

She'd thought to go back to Phoenix, because school and her apartment were there. But the idea of returning to the empty apartment was unbearable. If she went back, she'd have several weeks before the semester started, and she'd have nothing to do but sit and mope. And sink into despair.

On an impulse, she asked prices and distances to Kansas City, and discovered the trip was manageable. She could put the ticket on her credit card and use public transportation or a ride-sharing service when she got there.

It wasn't in the budget, but it felt like the right thing to do. Or at least, *a* thing to do. One more effort at atonement.

Four hours later she was on a bus north, riding through the night to Kansas City and a piece of her past.

* * *

As had happened before, Carson's twins were the saving of him.

Distraught as he was about what he'd learned about Pam, and about the vast secret Lily had kept from him, he still had to get up the next morning. Had to put on his game face and pack up their things and drive back to town.

Had to answer his girls' questions about why Miss Lily wasn't coming back.

"But she didn't say bye to us," Sunny protested when Carson said she'd had to go home.

"Is she mad?" Skye asked.

He shook his head. "No. She told me to tell you she loved spending Christmas with you," he said. It was a little modification of what she'd said—she'd said she loved them, plain and simple—but he felt funny saying that to the girls, when they'd probably never see her again.

He probably wouldn't, either.

Almost involuntarily, he brushed his fingertips with his thumb, remembering the feel of Lily's hair. He'd touched it only a couple of times, but it had been so soft and wispy.

He'd held her only the once, but the feeling was imprinted in his arms. Her delicacy, her slender strength.

He wouldn't feel those things again.

Wouldn't be as open to a woman, either. Not when it hurt this much to lose her. He'd always thought he'd eventually remarry, once he processed Pam's death and healed from it.

But the healing would be more difficult than he'd expected because of what he'd learned.

He doubted he'd remarry now. So this was how it would be: him ushering the girls out of the car—alone. Carrying their things inside their house—alone.

He could do single parenthood. He'd been doing it, and he could continue.

His reassurances had satisfied Sunny, but Skye was more sensitive. Spending the night at Long John's, and then coming home to an absent Miss Lily and a haggard, silent daddy, had upset her.

As they carried the last of their things back into their own house, he caught her wiping tears.

Carson dropped his load of suitcases and grocery bags right inside the front door and knelt to give her a hug. "What's wrong, muffin?" he asked.

"I wanted a mommy," she said into his shoulder, sniffling.

Carson's heart twisted, hard, and he tightened his arms around her. "I know you did. I'm sorry it didn't work out with Miss Lily."

Sunny shrugged. "Maybe someday, we'll meet someone else who can be the mommy of our family."

"But I liked *her*." The corners of Skye's mouth turned down.

Carson wrapped her in a big hug. "Me, too, baby. Me, too."

Fortunately, being kids, Sunny and Skye were quickly swept back into their town life of playmates and kindergarten and church activities.

Carson had a harder time of it. The days dragged by, even though he was immediately busy with the church. When he wasn't working, he looked at old pictures of Pam and wondered whether, even through her smiles, she'd been contemplating taking her own life. He tried to understand what might have led her to that pass. Wondered how much of it was his fault.

As it happened, he spent a fair amount of time counseling Gavin's family members. To be effective at it, he forced himself to read up on the subject of suicide, to understand the reasons for it. Despair, mental illness, hopelessness… Yeah. Pam had all of that.

If any good could come out of this awful situation, it was making him a better pastor. He could speak to Gavin's mom with real sympathy and understanding now, and she was doing better.

She felt terrible remorse for her actions. She agreed immediately with one of the catchphrases he'd shared with her: that taking one's own life was a permanent solution to a temporary problem.

Maybe Pam would have changed her mind, too, if she'd had time to think.

After a couple of weeks of ruminating about Pam, trying to process what she'd done, thoughts of Lily began to creep back into his mind. He attempted to push them away, tried to maintain his anger, threw himself into his work.

On an unseasonably warm and sunny Sunday toward the end of January, Jack and Finn suggested they take advantage of the weather by doing some outdoor projects at the church after services. Since the twins had gone home with some friends for a playdate, Carson decided to join the other two men.

Better than going home alone.

They talked football championships for a while, and then somehow, they moved into more emotional ground. "I didn't think Lily would leave," Jack said, his voice casual, conversational. "She seemed like the type who'd stay. She fit in real well here."

"I thought so, too," Carson said. "But she kept a few secrets."

"What do you mean?"

As they worked on a fence around the church's new playground, Carson told his friend some of what Lily had revealed about Pam.

Jack shook his head. "That's rough," he said when Carson had finished the sorry tale. "I know how it goes. You're asking yourself why, what you could have done differently. That news just dumped a whole lot of guilt on you, but you can't let it. Suicide's complicated. And who's to say she was thinking when she did it? She could've been trying to get out of serving and come home."

Finn, who was listening from the other side of the yard, gave Jack a look.

Jack glared right back. "I know you're a war hero, but not everyone's like that. Some people get themselves injured on purpose so they can come home. Maybe that was Pam."

"Humph." Finn went over to a different side of the fence to work.

"*Could* it have been an accident?" Jack asked.

"Nope," Carson said. "There was a note. Lily had it." He paused. "She had it all along, but she didn't see fit to tell me until I forced the issue."

"Whoa."

They worked in silence for a while longer. Then Jack spoke. "Lily didn't keep that information from you for a bad reason. She knew it would hurt you, right? She was trying to spare you pain."

"I guess."

"So maybe you should talk to her." Then Jack lifted his hands like stop signs. "Although, don't listen to me. I know nothing about love. Never going there again."

"Never?" Carson was genuinely curious. He didn't know much about Jack's past, aside from the fact that he'd unexpectedly lost his wife at a young age, right after they'd adopted a baby.

"Never." Jack shook his head. "Me and women don't get along."

Finn carried a load of planks over their way. "If you like Lily, go after her. Don't get caught up in stubborn pride, like I did. I almost lost Kayla and Leo because of it."

Carson remembered those days, when Finn had spiraled into darkness caused by his past tragedy, and Kayla and Leo had packed up to leave the ranch. It had almost had a disastrous outcome, but with God's help, Finn and Kayla had overcome their hurdles and built a happy life together.

Funny how much easier it was to see that happen in others than to believe it could happen for him.

"Listen, Carson." Jack glanced over at Finn, who came to stand beside him. "Even before what you said today, we…well, we were thinking you should talk to someone about Pam."

He leveled a glare at them. "Who's we? And talk to who?"

"Us," Finn said. "We think you should talk to a counselor."

"Because you're miserable," Jack said.

"And you pushed a good woman away," Finn added. Jack pulled out his phone. "I called around. There are a couple counselors in the area who might be able to help."

"I can find my own therapist!" Carson narrowed his eyes at the pair. "How long have you been planning this conversation?"

They glanced at each other and shrugged at the same moment.

"I'm sending you names," Jack said. "Call somebody, man. Talk to someone."

"Do it." Finn, the taciturn giant, took a step closer and glared at Carson.

"Fine, I'll call," he groused as Jack's information pinged into his phone. But even through his annoyance at their interference, Carson felt grateful for friends who cared enough to do it.

Chapter Fourteen

After paying the Uber driver, Lily stood in the lightly falling snow and stared at her old home in Kansas City. Once a nice neighborhood, the area had gone downhill in recent years, with more people leaving their lawns uncared for and bars on many windows. For all that, a lump came into her throat.

This had been home to her. She'd ridden her bike up and down the street, had climbed the apple tree that still remained in the front yard. She'd sat on those porch steps, banished to them while her father and mother had it out inside. She'd brought stacks of library books home and read them, getting lost in another world.

This had also been her base of operations when she'd gone so wild as a teenager. She'd been the kid whose parents didn't check into things too closely, which gave her house appeal as a party spot.

But there had been good times with her parents, if her dad was home and sober and her mom was over whatever hurt or anger he'd last inflicted on her. She remembered building a snowman with both of them when she was barely as tall as the porch railing, how her father had lifted her up to put in the snowman's carrot nose.

Just as she'd done with Carson's twins.

The thought of the girls made her throat tighten. And the thought of Carson brought downright misery.

She'd handled everything wrong. She should have told him the truth right away. Yes, she'd been trying to prevent his being hurt, but it had all backfired so badly.

In the end, she'd been to blame for Pam's death. There was no way to get around that.

And there was no way Pam's husband and daughters could love someone who'd done something so awful.

Despair threatened to crush her down, down, down onto the snowy, broken sidewalk, so she did as her army therapist had always told her to do: she concentrated on now. She walked the neighborhood, knocking on doors of homes whose occupants she remembered, asking questions. If she could find her father, maybe she could help him. Do for him what she hadn't been able to do for Pam.

An hour later, she hadn't gotten a single lead, and she stood staring at her old house again. Down the street, children played. A car door slammed. Lily bit her lip and pondered what to do next. Had this trip been a mistake?

"Is it what you remembered?"

Lily spun to the familiar voice. "Aunt Penny! What are you doing here?"

Penny put an arm around her and smiled. "When you called to see if I had an address for your dad, I figured you'd come here searching for him. I had a day before I had to get back to the ranch, and some frequent flyer miles, so…it was easy to come."

"That was so kind of you!" Tears welled in Lily's eyes. She'd never have expected her aunt to go so far out of her way for her.

"Just making up for what I wish I'd done years ago," Penny said matter-of-factly, looking around. "Your father doesn't still live here?"

"No. It's listed under a different owner." Lily gave Penny a quick hug, then turned to face the house. "I was just thinking about all the times we had here, good and bad. I remember when you came to visit, too."

Aunt Penny shook her head. "I should have come more. Your mom wasn't strong enough to give you what you needed. I wish I'd stepped in, even taken you to live with me."

"She wouldn't have allowed it," Lily said automatically, and realized that it was true. For all her mother's complaints and criticisms, she would never have let Lily be raised by anyone but her.

And that meant that her mother had loved her, even if she'd been too troubled to show it all the time.

"Any clues about your dad's whereabouts?" Penny asked.

"Not yet. The neighbors I remember don't live here anymore."

"What about him?" Penny pointed at a burly, white-haired African American man who'd just come around the side of the house next door, pushing a snowblower. His was one of the few cleaned-off driveways on the street.

"I don't think I know him, but—"

"But he might know something about your dad."

"Let's go ask."

The man shut down his snowblower and greeted them with a friendly smile, and after they'd all introduced themselves, Lily explained who they were looking for.

"I sure do remember him," the man, Mr. Ross, said, smiling more broadly as he shook his head a little. "Quite a character."

"So you know him!" Hope rose in Lily's heart.

"Any idea where he's living now?" Penny asked.

"Not sure," the man admitted. "But he was attending a program at the Church of the Redeemer, downtown. They might know more."

"He goes to church?" Lily couldn't restrain her surprise. While she and her mother had occasionally attended church during Lily's childhood, her father had adamantly refused to go along.

A smile curved up the man's face. "I wouldn't say he was attending steady, but he seemed to be moving in that direction. We had a few talks, he and I. He was lonely after losing his wife, looking for comfort in a bottle. We talked about how maybe there was a better way, and I pointed him toward their drug and alcohol program."

"Thank you." Lily reached out and grasped both of the man's hands. "I'm his daughter, and I so appreciate your reaching out."

"It's what we're called to do, isn't that right?" He smiled at her, then bent to start his snowblower again. "God bless you," he said over the sound of the motor.

"And you as well." If she found her father, then maybe some good would come out of this heartbreaking Christmas.

* * *

At the entrance to the downtown church, Lily froze.

Down the hall was a hunched figure, hair standing out crazily from his head, draped in a blanket that had maybe once been white. He stood at what looked like an intake desk, talking intently with the worker who sat there. The worker spoke back and finally appeared to be convinced; he stood, walked around the table and embraced the hunched man. Then they walked farther down the hall together.

The man's familiar gait convinced her of what she'd suspected, and her throat tightened. "That's him," she choked out in a whisper.

She gripped Penny's arm until the two men were out of sight. Then she turned to her aunt. "He's a street person. My father's on the streets."

Compassion crinkled Penny's eyes. "What do you want to do?"

Lily walked over to a chair in the church's entryway and sank down. "I want to help him. But how, when he's fallen this low?"

Penny sat beside her. "That man caused you and your mother a world of pain."

Lily nodded, releasing her breath in a shuddering sigh. "But he's my dad. And I can't believe he's here, in a shelter, looking like *that*…" She gestured in the direction her father had gone. "I feel terrible that I let it get to this point."

Penny shook her head impatiently. "No. This isn't your fault, and I'm not going to let you sit here and take responsibility."

"But he's my father. I could have tried harder to get him to come live with me." She'd invited him twice, once right after Mom had died and once a couple of months ago, but he'd refused both times.

And *she'd* refused to send him money instead, as he'd requested. She'd figured it would just go to alcohol, but maybe she'd been wrong.

"Your mother spent thirty years trying to fix that man. It's not something a human being can do. Only one way to heal that hurt, and we're in the place it can happen." Penny gestured around at the church. "Your dad probably hit bottom after your mom died, and maybe that's what he needed to do. That can be a step on the road. It's in God's hands."

The worker who'd disappeared with her father now came back, skirting the desk and coming toward them. "My name's Fred Jenson. Can I help you ladies?"

Lily glanced over at Penny, who was looking back at her, one eyebrow raised. Penny was leaving it up to her, and Lily was grateful. "We'd like to see Donny Watkins, if that's possible," she said. "I'm his daughter."

"Of course! He seems to be back on the upswing again. You could join us for a meal if you'd like." Fred gestured toward the back of the church. "We're serving lunch in our Fellowship Hall, and it's open to everyone."

"Maybe just a chat with Donny?" Penny looked over at Lily.

"Yes," Lily decided. "And we'll make a donation."

Fred smiled. "That's always appreciated. This way."

He led them into a room that held many people milling around, some dressed in the ragged layers of the homeless, a few families and some individuals bustling around with serving dishes, apparently workers or volunteers.

Fred seated them at the end of a long table. "I'll get Donny," he said, and disappeared.

Lily's stomach started dancing. She shot up a quick prayer for strength and the right words.

Minutes later, her father walked into the room. When he saw Lily, his whole face lit up.

He's glad to see me? Lily stood, barely knowing what she was doing.

They walked toward each other and both paused for a few seconds at arm's length. Lily took in his greasy shoulder-length hair, his stained shirt, his bloodshot eyes.

He looked like everything Lily's mother had spent her life trying to prevent, making him shower and dress in freshly ironed shirts, covering for him by calling him in sick to employers, working two jobs herself, at times, to pay the mortgage on their property.

She'd worked and stressed herself to death, and yet in the end, the outcome for her father was the same. He'd slid down the slippery slope on which he'd spent his whole life.

"Dad," she said, her voice catching, and held out her arms.

He took two long steps and pulled her into a tight hug. She almost choked on his body odor, but at least she didn't smell booze.

Then he stepped back, his hands on her shoulders. "Look at you," he said, smiling. "You've grown up to be everything your mother and I always hoped you'd be."

Lily's brow wrinkled and she shook her head. "You guys talked about my future?"

"We sure did. She always thought you'd be a writer, and I thought an artist."

"I'm a photographer, finishing up school," she said through a tight throat. The idea that her parents had talked about her, had dreams for her, touched her beyond measure.

"And you did real well in the military, too. I sure am proud of you." He took her hand and drew her to a sofa in the parlor. "You were what held us together, you know."

She sat down beside him and gestured Penny to an adjacent armchair, and they spent a half hour catching up. It turned out her father had been in this Christian rehab program for a month, except for falling off the wagon a few days ago. He'd gotten himself sober and come back.

"They allow one relapse, and that was mine," he explained. "I can't mess up again. Seeing you makes me motivated to keep my nose clean."

Penny mostly listened, but Lily was the one to probe about his plans, asking about the length of the program and what might come of it.

"We're one day at a time," Dad said, "but after six weeks, I need to start looking for a job and a place to stay. Move on, to make room for the next guy."

"Do they have aftercare, job counseling, stuff like that?"

"Yes, or if you want to move to another part of the country, they help you connect with a program there." He glanced speculatively at Lily.

"I'm sorry I didn't help you more," Lily said, fighting back tears. "I want you to get better. I wish there had been something I could do—"

Her father held up a hand. "Whoa. You're not responsible for me. You made efforts and offers and I turned you down." He shook his head. "I wasn't ready to live like a decent person then. Not sure I'm ready now, but maybe someday…"

Lily squeezed his hand, too moved to speak, too confused. Was this how they'd leave it, then? Would he make it or relapse again?

It was Penny who spoke up. "There might be a spot for a maintenance worker at the ranch I'm running," she said. "You're a veteran, right, Donny?"

"Navy man," he said proudly. "That's what drew your mother to me," he added to Lily. "She saw me in my dress whites and that was that."

Lily smiled through her weepiness, remembering the oft-told story.

"There's no alcohol at the ranch," Penny warned, "but there's a bunkhouse we're working on that could be a place for you to stay awhile. When you're ready." She put an arm around Lily. "This one has dreams to dream and a life to live, but I'm hoping she'll settle in Colorado. It would be nice if you were in the same area, at least."

Penny's protectiveness made Lily swallow hard.

"I always wanted to see the West," her father said. "Maybe it'll happen." He turned to Lily. "I sure would like to make amends for the kind of father I was."

She shook her head. "No amends needed," she said, meaning it. But his words made her think.

She'd always blamed herself for the difficulties her mother and father had faced, and the fact was, her mom had sometimes blamed her, too. It was what had pushed Lily into acting out as a younger woman, living the wild, partying lifestyle she now regretted.

But maybe it hadn't been entirely her fault after all.

"Sorry to interrupt," came a voice at the door. "It's almost time for lunch, and you're on serving duty, Donny."

He stood immediately. "I need to get myself cleaned up."

Lily stood, too, and held out her arms. "I'm so glad you're finding your way," she said to him. "And I hope you do come to Colorado and work at the ranch. It's an amazing place."

All of a sudden she heard what she'd said. *Come* to Colorado. As if she'd be there herself. But she'd left, run away, broken off the relationships she had there. Hadn't she?

After an emotional goodbye, Lily spent a few minutes composing herself in the ladies' room and then met Penny in the parking lot.

"Where's next?" Penny asked. "I could take you to lunch before my plane leaves. In fact, those frequent flyer miles are burning a hole in my pocket, so if you'd like to fly back to Colorado with me…it's a lot faster than the bus."

Again, Penny's motherliness made Lily's throat tight.

"Seriously," Penny urged. "Come back with me, at least for a visit. If not permanently."

"I…I'd like that," Lily said. "Thank you. And I'm sorry, I'm not usually so weepy."

"Makes sense, on an emotional day." Penny put an arm around her. "Heard you left the ranch. Was it a good visit?"

"The best," Lily said fervently.

"Any chance you'll stay on in the area? I'd be glad to have you. And sounds like maybe your dad will be there, too, at some point."

"I love it there," she said. "But—" She broke off. Where to start?

Penny gestured Lily into the car and went around to the driver's side. "Get in. We'll talk."

Once they were heading toward the airport, Penny glanced over at her. "I spoke with Carson."

"Oh…" Lily said the word on a sigh. "How is he? How are the girls?"

"Everyone's managing. Missing you."

Lily frowned. "Did he say that?"

"Not in so many words, but I know him. I read between the lines."

Lily tried to process the tsunami of emotions inside her. Sadness, happiness, longing. And love. For her father. For Penny. And maybe, for Carson and his girls.

At the airport, Penny pulled into a parking space and turned off the car. "I'd be tickled to have you come live on the ranch, or in Esperanza Springs," she said. "I'd like to get to know you better as an adult. Seems to me you've grown into a very special person."

That warmed Lily's heart. "I do love it there," she said, propping her elbows on her knees, looking out the icy window. "But I don't want to make Carson's life difficult. His girls…they were getting attached to me, and I to them. It wouldn't be right."

"Those girls need a whole lot of mother figures. I'm one of them. What's wrong with you playing that role, too?"

"You don't understand. I…I really hurt Carson. I

knew his wife, see. And there were things I didn't tell him about her death."

"Huh."

A plane was taking off, lifting into the air with the elegance of a giant silver bird. Behind them, a family pulled luggage from a car's trunk, then headed toward the terminal, each pulling a suitcase.

"Is there any chance," Penny asked, "that you're carrying baggage that's not yours to carry?"

Lily tilted her head to one side, considering.

"Blame you're taking on for something that isn't your fault? Like you did with your parents?"

Was she doing that?

What if she weren't to blame for Pam's death, despite what Pam had said? Lily had done the best she could, given that the investigators had asked her direct questions. And she hadn't just been tattling; Pam's drug use while on duty had put a lot of people at risk.

Maybe she'd been right to say the truth. Even if what Pam had done with the results was purely horrible.

Lily had been wrong to keep information from Carson. A mistake, for sure, maybe even a self-protective sin. It wasn't likely that he'd forgive her.

But was it possible? As they walked into the airport, she thought about Carson, the girls and the town of Esperanza Springs. The ranch and Long John.

She did want it, all of it, if she were honest with herself. She wanted the closeness that she'd started to feel with Carson. She wanted to be near him and help him and care for him, and be cared for in return. Wanted to make a family with him and his girls.

It wasn't likely to work out, no—but it wasn't impossible. Maybe at some point in the future, they could reconnect.

Did she have the emotional strength to go back there again, to talk with him, apologize for the secrets, talk through what had happened to Pam? To try again, knowing she might fail, was actually likely to fail?

But something about today, the reconciliation with her father, the help Penny had offered so freely, had strengthened her. Or maybe just reminded her of the strength she already had. She turned to her aunt. "I have to tie up some loose ends at school and in Phoenix," she said. "But if you have space on the ranch, in a month or so, I'd like to come stay for a little while," she said. "I'll work to earn my keep."

Chapter Fifteen

Carson did *not* want to go back up to Redemption Ranch. His whole heart rebelled against it.

But he had to break the ice, jump in the water, get back on the horse. Whatever cliché you wanted to use, he had to do it. Somehow. It had been almost six weeks since Lily had left. His life and the girls' lives were back to normal. And for him, normal included serving as chaplain at the ranch.

Finn had let him know they were expecting more veterans soon, so Carson had to get used to going up there. He had to harden himself to being in the place where he'd fallen in love and lost his dream.

Those six weeks had been busy for him, because he had realized all the things he needed to work out. On the practical side, he had talked to army officials about Pam's discharge status and gotten a fuller picture of what had happened on the last day of her life, as well as the weeks leading up to it.

The information he'd received had been distressing, but in a way, not a surprise. He had known about most of Pam's issues. They had just gotten worse during her last weeks, when she'd stopped taking her medication and everything had gone wrong.

Carson had his own guilt to deal with. He knew why she'd gone off her meds: because she was pregnant. He wished he had considered that and talked to her about it, but he had been caught up in the joy of expecting another baby and the concern about her serving in the military while pregnant, and he hadn't stopped to think about the mental health issues involved.

Stupid, stupid, stupid.

Fortunately, he had good friends in Finn and Jack. And he had taken their advice and consulted someone who could help: not a therapist, but an older pastor who had lots of experience with similar issues. According to all of these men, his mistake was a mistake, not a sign that he was hopelessly and fatally flawed. According to them, the responsibility for taking the meds, or talking to a physician about how to go off them, ultimately rested on Pam.

Still, he'd struggled to understand, had wrestled with the issue in prayer. But the verse that kept coming to him was about seeing through a glass darkly now. Clarity might never come until he himself joined his Father in heaven, saw Him face-to-face and also saw the whole truth of life.

"Daddy, Daddy, we're almost there!"

"Do you think our doggy will be like Rockette or like Shoney?" Shoney, the cocker spaniel Finn had adopted right along with Leo, when he'd married Kayla, had plenty of challenges. But they did nothing to dampen her spirit, and everyone in Esperanza Springs loved her.

"Long John said we would like her," Carson reminded the girls. "What she's like will be a surprise. I'm excited, too."

And he was, as hard as that was to believe. In the midst of all his other self-realizations, he'd come to understand that the reason he didn't want a dog had more to do with his parents and the way he was raised than with any actual dislike of having a pet. Once he'd figured that out, he had been glad for Jack and Long John to get the girls a dog.

"Remember," he said as he pulled the truck into the gravel space in front of Long John's cabin. "We're just meeting this pooch. If she isn't right for us, there will be another dog who is."

"I hope it's her," Skye said, her forehead wrinkling. "If we meet her and don't like her, she'll feel very sad."

"Come on, come on!" Sunny was already unbuckling her seat belt, and as soon as Carson turned off the truck, she opened the door and rushed outside. Skye wasn't far behind her.

As they tromped up Long John's steps, Carson's eyes strayed toward the cabin where Lily had stayed, and immediately his mind was filled with thoughts and images of her. How they had spent Christmas Eve right here, at Long John's. How they'd built a snowman with the girls, watched them go sledding, just over the hill.

But his girls needed him to be present now rather than reminiscing about the past, and so he shoved those thoughts aside and climbed the steps after them. Before they could even pound on the door, Long John opened it, and then the girls were inside with a fuzz-ball of energy like he had never seen before.

He tilted his head to the side and watched as the

girls shrieked and rolled on the floor with the light brown fuzzball.

Fuzzballs.

He glanced over at Long John. "There are two of them."

"You have two girls."

"Yeah, but…"

Long John laughed. "You have to admit, it's a good surprise. For them and for you."

"For them, anyway." Carson blew out a sigh. How much more work could two dogs be than one? "What kind of dogs are they, anyway? I've never seen anything like them."

"Jack called 'em sporgis, or some such fool thing," Long John said. "A boy and a girl, some crazy mix of spaniel and corgi."

The dogs were, indeed, fluffy like some breeds of spaniels he'd seen. But their bodies were long and low-slung, corgi-like.

"Aren't they pretty, Daddy?" Skye looked up at him, her eyes glowing.

Carson was saved from having to answer by Sunny's giggles as her dog, an exact replica of her brother, barreled into her lap and started to lick her face.

"You'd better not have any other surprises up your sleeve," Carson warned Long John.

Long John didn't answer. Instead, he pushed his walker to the window and looked out. "Jack DeMoise was planning to come up so he could show you some things about taking care of them," he said. "Wonder where he is."

Carson came over to join him at the window. He looked out at the snowy landscape, then down toward the cabins where he, the girls and Lily had spent Christmas.

Again, memories assailed him. They'd had such a good time together. That warmth and caring between them had been real.

He'd been a real jerk to get angry with Lily for what Pam had done. He knew that now.

When a figure came into view, at first, he couldn't believe his eyes. Petite, royal blue jacket, wheat-blond hair fluffed out around a face he'd feared he'd never see again... Had he conjured Lily up out of his own imagination?

He turned to look at Long John. "Is that..." He trailed off.

The older man chuckled. "Surprise," he said.

Lily pushed the cabin door open. She didn't like to make Long John get up if he didn't need to.

She had been back at the ranch just a couple of days, but aside from the pain she felt every time she looked at the cabin where Carson and the girls had stayed, the place felt wonderful, like home. She had spent time with Penny, hammering out a job description that would let her help with the dogs, do PR for the ranch and still give her time to work on her exciting new project.

What her dad had said, how he and Mom had always thought she would end up in a creative profession, had impacted her. She had finished and turned in her thesis, and the feedback she had received had been so positive that she had decided to try to turn it into a book.

She was checking messages on her phone, so she

barely looked up as she walked into Long John's cabin. "Hey, are you ready for me to take those dogs down to the kennel?"

"Not quite." There was laughter in the old man's voice.

"Miss Lily!" No sooner had she heard the words, the voices she'd missed so terribly, than the twins were flinging themselves on her. She sank down to her knees to properly hug the girls, inhaling their sweaty, soapy scent, listening to their excited greetings, her eyes closed.

She hardly dared look up, because if the twins were here, then… She took a deep breath and opened her eyes.

There was Carson.

The sight of him rocked her like an earthquake.

What was he doing here? Why were the girls here? And most important, did he want to see her, or was this as surprising and even upsetting to him as it was to her?

She looked away, overcome with feeling, and then made herself look back up at him to discover that he was staring at her. Looking serious.

There was another knock on the door. "Come on in," Long John called, and the door opened to Jack DeMoise.

"Everyone ready to go down to the kennel and collect the paperwork and supplies for these two pups?" Jack looked around the room and smiled. "I'm assuming our plan was a success?"

"That remains to be seen." Long John made his way across the room toward Jack. "Come on, girls," he said. "Let's take the dogs down and start gathering up their things. That way, we can give your daddy and Miss Lily a few minutes alone."

Only then did the girls let go of Lily. Sunny ran to the door, ready to go anywhere as long as her new dog went with her. But Skye stood still, looking from Lily to her father. "Are you guys going to fight?"

"No, I don't think so," Lily said softly. "But we do have a few things to talk about."

She wanted to tell Carson how sorry she was. Wanted to hear what he was thinking, although from the serious expression still on his face, she didn't have much hope that he was feeling positive toward her.

There was a moment of flurry and chaos as Long John, Jack, the twins and the two strange-looking dogs headed out the door. And then it closed, and there was silence.

Feeling awkward, Lily got to her feet and walked over to the kitchen area, leaning her back against the counter. She didn't look directly at Carson. If she did, he would see her feelings in her eyes, and she didn't want the humiliation of that. Not when he didn't feel the same.

Besides, she needed to lean on something, because the very sight of him made her weak in the legs, like she might fall over. She still felt everything she had felt for him before. In fact, when you added in the realizations she'd had and the thinking she'd done in the past month, she felt even more.

"Lily." Carson cleared his throat. "I wasn't expecting to see you here today, but I *was* hoping to see you. I have a lot to say and an apology to make."

"About what?" She tried, unsuccessfully, to sound casual.

"I was judgmental before. I didn't understand anything."

Lily sucked in a breath.

He came to stand across from her, just an arm's length away, and his closeness squeezed at her heart. She'd been getting stronger, she knew that, but being in the same room with Carson was undoing her.

"I've been doing a lot of thinking about Pam," he said. "And a lot of talking to other people about her."

"You have?" Her voice came out husky, and she cleared her throat.

"I talked to her parents."

She cocked her head to one side. "You *did*? Don't they live overseas?" And if she recalled correctly, they hadn't been good to Pam.

He nodded. "I was able to track them down in the South of France. I found out something that shifted what I'd been thinking. It might shift your view, too."

"Okay." She squeezed her hands into fists.

"There's no easy way to say this." He sighed, then met Lily's eyes. "She'd attempted to take her own life twice before, once as a teenager and once in her early twenties."

"What?" Lily stared at him.

He nodded. "I didn't know. She'd never mentioned it, and neither did they, the couple of times I saw them." He tilted his head, watching her. "It wasn't about anything you did, Lily, no matter what she said, what the note said. I realize now that she lied a lot, and I think she lied about what was motivating her."

Lily let out her breath, her shoulders sagging.

"There were mental health issues all along, and imbalances that were at least partly chemical. Her medications were crucial," he went on, "but she had that rebellious streak. Her parents said they'd thrown up their hands about getting her to take her meds. And she concealed her need for them from her CO and her military doctors."

"Wow." Instinctively, she responded to the pain in Carson's voice. "That must be so hard to deal with."

"I didn't know how bad things could get inside her head. She was good at covering up, but I wish she hadn't felt she had to."

"I think…it wasn't under her control. Not entirely, anyway." Lily thought of her beautiful, wild friend. "If only I could have brought her closer to the Lord, maybe…"

He nodded. "I have the exact same regret. But, Lily, she *was* saved. She believed."

"And she's free now, free and happy." Lily's eyes filled with tears. "I wish she could have lived. For the girls to know."

"I'll make sure to keep talking about her as they grow," he said firmly. "All the good things about her, and there were a lot of them."

"There were." Lily's voice caught, and she grabbed a paper towel to blot her eyes. "There were."

They were both silent for a long moment. Lily was thinking of her friend, of her laughter and her beauty and her charm. What a terrible loss.

From the way Carson blinked and swallowed, she could tell he was having similar thoughts.

Finally, he walked over to the cupboard, pulled out two glasses and filled them with water. He handed one to her, and they both drank deeply.

"I'll always feel some guilt," he said. "But one thing

her death has made me realize is that life is short. Too short to waste it on petty misunderstandings." He drained his glass and put it in the sink. "I'm sorry to have blamed you for what she did. It wasn't your fault, and I'm sorry I acted as though it was."

She walked toward him then. Reached out and grasped his hands. "I hope that means you can forgive me. And that we can be…friends, maybe."

"Lily." He drew in a breath, audibly. "I hope we can be more than friends."

"More?" The word came out in a squeak.

He didn't smile, didn't laugh at her. Instead, he squeezed her hands just a little, and Lily felt it, the warmth of it, wash through her whole body. "I know we haven't had much time together, but I also know how I feel. You are the woman for me, Lily. I know that without a doubt. And I would very much like to explore a relationship with you. I'll wait, and we can take it slowly, because I know you're not there yet, but—"

Lily extracted one hand from his and held it up, her head spinning. "Wait. Rewind. Did you just say you want a relationship with me?"

"I did. I do."

"Because of the girls?"

He shook his head back and forth slowly, a gentle smile coming over his face. "I'm thrilled that the girls love you so much, but that's not the reason. You're kind, and beautiful, and you fascinate me. I want to get to know you, and keep getting to know you, for the rest of my life." He held up a hand. "I know I'm getting way ahead of myself. I know we're just starting to reconnect. But I can't help telling you that for me, this is it and this is real."

Lily's eyes filled with tears, and she took deep breaths, just trying to stay calm and absorb what he was saying.

He took a step closer. "I'm not even the jealous type, but I get jealous whenever I think of other men looking at you. Because I want you. I want you because of your smile and the way you treat other people and that strength you've shown to get through the hard times in your life." He tilted his head to one side and his eyes clouded. "Do I have a chance, Lily? Do you think that, with time, you might be able to come to care for me? Even to, maybe, become part of my family, with me and the girls?"

She couldn't restrain the tears now, not completely, and she felt one leak out down her cheek as she looked up at him. Neither could she restrain the smile that broke out across her face. "I care for you. A lot."

His expression brightened, sunshine after clouds. "That night when we kissed," he said, "you felt so right in my arms." He took a step toward her, and his hands cupped her face, a thumb brushing aside her tears. Gently, he lowered his face to hers and brushed her lips with his. "I know it's early and I know we have a lot to talk about, but…can we try?"

Her throat was too tight to speak, so she just nodded. And smiled. And wrapped her arms around his neck to pull him down and kiss him again.

Epilogue

Carson straightened his tie and checked his cuff links, then glanced once more at the clock.

"We're ready, Daddy!" Sunny and Skye came running into the kitchen of the parsonage, dressed in identical green Easter dresses. They'd worn them to church this morning and hadn't wanted to take them off, which had fit in just fine with Carson's plans.

Trouble was, he was now questioning those plans.

Lily was fifteen minutes late to the home-cooked Easter dinner, which wasn't like her.

"Look, Basie and Boomer are ready, too!" Skye squatted and clapped her hands, and Sunny released the two dogs into the kitchen, both sporting green ribbons around their thick necks.

The dogs were still a bit odd-looking, and the frilly bows didn't change that. But they'd made the girls ecstatically happy, and Carson found himself enjoying their antics, too, and not minding the extra work they created.

He felt calmer and more peaceful generally. He'd laid memories from the past to rest. More than that, he and the girls had been spending a lot of time with Lily, working toward a future together.

Tonight, he would cement that. If she ever showed up.

"There she is!" Sunny spotted something out the window and ran to open the door for Lily, who was weighed down with a big armload of packages.

"It's like Christmas again!" Sunny crowed, and Skye clasped her hands together, her eyes excited.

Lily gave them a big smile and then dumped her bag of presents out onto the couch. "Okay, girls, you need to figure out which ones are for you and which are for the dogs."

She'd written names on the labels, and Sunny and Skye immediately discovered their own names and, after a nod from Carson, tore in. "Summer pajamas!" Skye said, holding up a pretty cotton pair.

"Look at mine!" Sunny's were brighter and louder, just like the child herself.

"And there's a book, too!"

"In mine, too!"

Of course, she'd bought them books, too. She was such a good influence, encouraging them to learn and grow.

But mostly, she was a loving influence. The girls were becoming more confident in her affection, in the fact that she'd be a part of their future.

The trouble was, Carson still wasn't sure she'd be willing to make it permanent. But he didn't want to wait, and Easter seemed like the right time for new beginnings.

"What are these packages?" Skye asked, indicating two more large packages on the couch.

"Read the labels to find out," Lily said, and they studied the labels until they were able to read the dogs' names. "Open them," Lily urged, and the girls ripped in.

"Dog coats!" they cried and rushed to fit them on the dogs. Which had to be almost impossible, since the dogs were long like dachshunds, but bigger around.

"I made them," Lily confided, glancing up at Carson with a smile. "Because these dogs can't exactly do ready-to-wear."

"There's one more package, Daddy," Skye said, bringing over a flat package to Carson.

He lifted an eyebrow. "Should I open it?"

"Of course."

When he did, he couldn't believe his eyes. It was a framed photo of him, the girls and Lily on the sledding hill, that first Christmas they'd spent together. "Where did you get this?"

"Who knew that Long John was snapping photos with his camera?" She smiled at him. "I was so happy to see it. I thought you and the girls might like a copy, too."

It was the perfect segue into what he wanted to do. He pulled her toward the couch in front of the fire he'd built. "Sit down," he urged her, "so I can give you my Easter present."

"Oh, you didn't have to get me anything. I know you've been busy."

"Close your eyes!" the girls shouted.

"Well...okay." She did, and he and the twins got into position.

Carson's hands were sweating as he pulled the small

box out of his pocket, and he shot up a quick prayer: *Not my will, but Thine.*

And please, make our two wills go together this time.

He held the red velvet cushion they'd found at a thrift store and nodded to the girls. "Open your eyes," he said.

She did and stared at the red cushion with the little box in the center.

"Lily," he said formally, "we would like to ask you to be part of our family."

He nudged Sunny.

"You could be part of it just by being our friend," she said, as coached.

"Like an aunt," Skye said.

"But we hope you'll be our mom!" Sunny blurted the words out and then clapped her hand over her mouth. They weren't supposed to put pressure on her.

"Now you know what to do," he told the twins.

"Do we have to, Daddy?" Sunny asked.

"We have to!" Skye grabbed her twin's hand and tugged.

"You *might* find some Easter candy up in your room," Carson said.

That was motivation enough, and they ran upstairs.

Leaving him alone with Lily. And very insecure about what she might be thinking. He looked at her, still on his knees, trying to read her face. "I love you so much, Lily," he said. "You've shown me the way to a new life with more happiness than I ever dreamed I could have."

She pressed her hand to her mouth, looking at him, eyes shining with what looked like tears.

"I hope you'll be their mom, too," he said. "They love you so much. But most of all, I hope you'll be my wife."

She reached down to put her hands on his shoulders, then leaned forward to press her lips to his.

A moment later, his head spinning, he let go of her enough to pick up the ring box that had fallen to the floor. "You... Wow." He shot her a smile. "You didn't even see the ring yet. I hope you like it. I... Was that a yes?"

She laughed, a joyous sound, and then there was a clatter of footsteps on the stairs that told him their time alone was over.

He had to know. "Lily?"

"It's a yes," she said. "Oh, Carson, it's my dream come true."

And as his girls threw themselves on both of them, all giggling happiness, he looked over the two blond heads and met Lily's eyes. "It's my dream come true, too."

* * * * *

*Don't miss Finn and Kayla's story
in the first book of Lee Tobin McClain's
Redemption Ranch miniseries:*

The Soldier's Redemption

Available now from Love Inspired!

Find more great reads at www.LoveInspired.com

Dear Reader,

I love Christmas! Carols and decorations, kids' excitement, Christmas Eve services—all bring joy. And what better place to experience Christmas than at a snowy ranch in Colorado?

Lily and Carson do experience Christmas joy, but they have pain to overcome before they can open themselves to love. The loss of his wife, Lily's friend, leaves them both with unresolved issues to overcome.

The topic of suicide is a very painful one, but it is a reality that touches many lives, my own included. I have tried to portray fairly both the depth of misery that can lead someone to take their own life and the guilt that remains with survivors. Help *is* available: the National Suicide Prevention Lifeline, 1-800-273-8255, offers free and confidential support 24/7. As the gospel tells us in John 10:10, "I am come that they might have life, and that they might have it more abundantly."

That is my wish for you and yours in this Christmas season: abundant life.

Thank you for visiting Redemption Ranch! Sign up for my newsletter if you'd like notification when the next book comes out: www.leetobinmcclain.com.

Warm Christmas wishes,
Lee

*When a young Amish woman has amnesia during
the holidays, will a handsome Amish farmer help
her regain her memories?*

Read on for a sneak preview of
Amish Christmas Memories *by Vannetta Chapman,
available December 2018 from Love Inspired.*

"What's your name?"

The woman's eyes widened and her hand shook so that
she could barely hold the mug of tea without spilling it. She
set it carefully on the coffee table. "I don't—I don't know
my name."

"How can you not know your own name?" Caleb asked.
"Do you know where you live?"

"Nein."

"What were you doing out there?"

"Out where?"

"Where was your coat and your *kapp*?"

"Caleb, now's not the time to interrogate the poor girl."
His *mamm* stood and moved beside her on the couch. She
picked up the small book of poetry. "You were carrying this,
when Caleb found you. Do you remember it?"

"I don't. This was mine?"

"Found it in the snow," Caleb said. "Right beside where
you collapsed."

"So it must be mine."

Caleb noticed that the woman's hands trembled as she
opened the cover and stared down at the first page. With one
finger, she traced the handwriting there.

"Rachel. I think my name is Rachel."

Rachel let her fingers brush over the word again and again. Rachel. Yes, that was her name. She was sure of it. She remembered writing it in the front of the book—she'd used a pen that her *mamm* had given her. She could almost picture herself, somewhere else. She could almost see her mother.

"My *mamm* gave me the pen and the book…for my birthday, I think. I wrote my name—wrote it right here."

"Your *mamm*. So you remember her?"

"Praise be to *Gotte*," Caleb's *dat* said, a smile spreading across his face.

"Is there someone we can call? If you remember the name of your bishop…" Caleb had sat down in the rocker his mother had vacated and was staring at her intensely.

They all were.

She closed her eyes, hoping to feel the memory again. She tried to see the room or the house or the people, but the memory had receded as quickly as it had come, leaving her with a pulsing headache.

She struggled to keep the feelings of panic at bay. Her heart was hammering, and her hands were shaking, and she could barely make sense of the questions they were pelting at her.

Who were these people?

Where was she?

Who was she?

She needed to remember what had happened.

She needed to go home.

Don't miss
Amish Christmas Memories *by Vannetta Chapman,*
available December 2018 wherever
Love Inspired® books and ebooks are sold.

www.LoveInspired.com

Looking for inspiration in tales
of hope, faith and heartfelt romance?

Check out **Love Inspired®** and
Love Inspired® Suspense books!

New books available every month!

CONNECT WITH US AT:

Facebook.com/groups/HarlequinConnection

Facebook.com/HarlequinBooks

Twitter.com/HarlequinBooks

Instagram.com/HarlequinBooks

Pinterest.com/HarlequinBooks

ReaderService.com

Inspirational Romance to Warm Your Heart and Soul

Join our social communities to connect with other readers who share your love!

Sign up for the Love Inspired newsletter at **www.LoveInspired.com** to be the first to find out about upcoming titles, special promotions and exclusive content.

CONNECT WITH US AT:

Facebook.com/groups/HarlequinConnection

 Facebook.com/LoveInspiredBooks

 Twitter.com/LoveInspiredBks

LISOCIAL2018